CHERRY POPPER

Cherry #1

VICTORIA QUINN

Hartwick Publishing

Cherry Popper

Copyright © 2019 by Victoria Quinn

All rights reserved.

No part of this book may be reproduced in any form or by any electronic or mechanical means, including information storage and retrieval systems, without written permission from the author, except for the use of brief quotations in a book review.

Contents

1.	Monroe	1
2.	Monroe	9
3.	Slate	17
4.	Monroe	21
5.	Slate	33
6.	Monroe	39
7.	Slate	49
8.	Monroe	71
9.	Slate	79
10.	Monroe	91
11.	Slate	103
12.	Monroe	115
13.	Slate	123
14.	Monroe	131
15.	Slate	147
16.	Monroe	169
17.	Slate	177
18.	Monroe	195
19.	Slate	213
20.	Monroe	233
21.	Slate	241
22.	Monroe	247
23.	Slate	277

Also by Victoria Quinn — 295

1

Monroe

It was that time of the month.

Bills.

I dreaded picking up the mail in the lobby of my apartment building because that was the only thing waiting in my box. Bills and pizza coupons.

The pizza coupons were the only thing I had to look forward to.

Because I was definitely eating on a budget.

I sat at the kitchen table in my apartment and opened each envelope.

The first was a bill for my student loan for my undergrad. The second was a bill for my masters. The third was a medical bill. And then I had to worry about the other essentials, like electricity and water. After deducting all my bills from my paycheck, I was left with a hundred bucks.

I had to survive for the next two weeks on a hundred bucks.

Jesus Christ.

I stared at the papers around me and felt the hopelessness inside my chest. The reason I'd gone to college was so I could have a good job someday. Now I was a marketing executive for a clothing company. I had a great salary and benefits. But the job was in Manhattan, so I had to live in the city—which cost a fortune on its own. With all my other bills, I was broke. I was living just to pay bills at this point.

So much for the American dream.

I would move out of the city and commute, but I couldn't afford a car. I couldn't even afford a down payment on one. I could move to Brooklyn or Queens, but having a decent apartment was the one luxury I wanted to maintain.

But if I wanted food, I'd have to give it up.

And I did like food…a lot.

I hated to sit around and feel sorry for myself, but tonight, that was impossible. This would be the next twenty years of my life, working to pay bills. I would work forty hours a week just to come home and eat crackers, sleep, and then do it all over again. I didn't even have enough money to go out on the weekends. I would never find a guy to spend my life with because he would run the second he heard how much debt I had.

And I couldn't blame him. I would do the exact same thing.

Cherry Popper

"YOU AREN'T GOING to order anything?" Cindy sat across from me at the table in the deli. We both worked in the same office, so we took our breaks together at the same time. She worked in accounting.

"Not hungry." I just sipped my water and thought about the crackers I would eat at my desk when I returned.

"Are you sure there's nothing wrong?" she asked. "You've been down all week."

Because I was drowning in debt. "Do you have a roommate?"

"Uh…yes. Why?"

"I'm looking for a roommate. And a new apartment. I just can't afford my place anymore."

"I have three roommates, actually."

"Three?" I asked incredulously. "Are you in a townhouse?"

"No. Two-bedroom apartment. Two girls per bedroom."

Oh my god, they were like rats. "Seriously? What do you do when you bring a guy around?"

"Go to his place," she said. "There's just not enough room there. Only one bathroom."

That sounded like a nightmare. "How much do you pay in rent?"

"A thousand."

My jaw dropped. "You pay a thousand dollars for that?"

She nodded. "It's all I can afford. How much do you pay for yours?"

"Two thousand…but it's too expensive. I can't swing it anymore."

"What are you talking about? You must make at least $70,000 a year."

"Yeah…but I have a ton of student loans. Even if I were only paying a thousand dollars in rent, I would still be drowning." I left out the part about the medical expenses, which I would be paying off until the day I died.

"That's too bad," she said. "I had a friend who was in a really tight spot. She was so desperate, she sold her virginity to Slate Remington."

I heard every word she said, but it took a few seconds to actually process it. "She sold her virginity…? People still do that?"

"Yep." She picked up her sandwich with both hands and took a bite. "And she got a fat check for it."

"How much?"

"A hundred thousand."

My jaw dropped again. "He paid that much for it?"

She nodded. "That's his thing. They call him the Cherry Popper."

"That's his thing?" I asked. "So, he does this on a regular basis?"

"That's what I hear."

The guy sounded like a huge douchebag, even if he paid well for the product. He was probably some rich asshole who had so much money he didn't know what to do with it—so he spent it on pussy. He could buy whores, but instead, he wanted something cleaner. But despite how much I despised it, I could really use that money… It would take away a good chunk of my debt. "What's his name again?"

"Slate Remington. You don't know who he is?"

"Am I supposed to know who he is?" I lived in my own world, focusing on getting through the day. I didn't have time to pay attention to rich playboys who spent their money on ridiculous things—like people.

"He's pretty well known. He owns all the Remington hotels and resorts."

I recognized the chain. It was a luxury line of resorts that existed all over the world, not that I could ever afford to stay in one.

"He owns a few other companies too," she said. "But I don't remember what they are."

I grabbed my phone and typed his name into Google, curious to see what he looked like. He was probably an older man with disgusting fetishes, a guy who couldn't get a girl growing up, so now he just paid for sex.

The search results popped up—and Slate Remington was nothing like I thought he would be.

Young.

Handsome.

Fit.

Sexy.

He did not look like a man who had to pay for sex. "This is him?" I held up the phone.

"Yep. Sexy, right?"

"Super sexy." I pulled the phone back to me. "I'm surprised this guy wastes his money like that. He must get ass handed to him all the time."

"Probably. But every guy has his kinks. Why are you so interested?"

Because I was desperate and pathetic. "Just curious…"

Cindy didn't press me on it. "His brother owns a bunch of companies too, but I guess they haven't spoken in a long time. He's private about his life. The only reason why I know he's the Cherry Popper is because my friend told me. But I guess she wasn't supposed to mention that…"

"Well, it doesn't make him look very good."

"I doubt he cares. A man that rich and good-looking probably doesn't care what people think of him."

"Yeah…probably not." I looked at his Wikipedia page and saw that he was thirty, fairly young to have so much success.

He was seven years older than me—and a million times more experienced. I locked the screen on my phone then looked out the window again, unable to believe I was even considering this.

It was so degrading.

Would I really give up my V-card for money?

If I weren't up to my eyeballs in debt, I wouldn't be enticed by the money. But my future would be infinitely more difficult if I carried all that debt. I could never start a family because I wouldn't be able to provide for them. I would be too tied up in my loans. Maybe I shouldn't have gone to college and should have just stayed in Connecticut. I could have started at a bank and worked my way up. I wouldn't have any loans, and the rent would be cheaper. Honestly, I was probably better off going that route than taking out hundreds of thousands in student loans.

I wish I could go back in time and redo it all.

Or I could give up my virginity and make my life a little easier.

2

Monroe

FOR THE NEXT WEEK, I CONTINUED TO DEBATE WITH myself.

Could I really do something like that?

My initial reaction was no, but once I saw what he looked like, it didn't seem so bad. He had short, dark hair, a masculine jawline, brown eyes that looked a little scary, and a muscular physique that must be perfectly manicured every single day. His suits fit his sculpted shoulders and arms like a second skin, and he was tall. Pictures could be deceptive, but anytime he was around other men, he was always the tallest one in the group.

Maybe it was immoral. Maybe it made me a skank.

But I needed to live.

And unless I won the lottery, that wasn't going to happen.

It would be an embarrassing story when I told my husband. He might think less of me for giving up my purity for a check. Or I could just keep it to myself and never tell another soul. No one would ever know.

But I hated keeping a secret like that.

By the end of the week, I only had twenty bucks in my account. I still needed to eat for another week, so that meant I would be dining on peanut butter and jelly sandwiches for every meal until I got paid.

That was all the convincing I needed. I couldn't live like this much longer, and if I had to get on my back for thirty minutes while an asshole fucked me, that seemed like a small compromise. I could pay off my undergraduate degree completely—and eliminate one loan payment altogether.

That would save me $1,000 a month. To someone like me, that was a fortune.

I was in a bad situation, and I didn't have the time to be noble or classy.

I had to survive.

And I wouldn't apologize for it.

I DID some research and found where his main office was located. It was the administrative building for his chain of resorts, and it was in Manhattan. I wasn't sure what to wear because it wasn't a job interview, but I didn't want to walk in looking like a prostitute either. I settled for a pencil skirt and blouse, something that outlined my curves but didn't give away too much. I did my hair and makeup then left for his office.

I didn't know how to go about this because I

couldn't tell his secretary exactly what I wanted. She probably knew nothing about his personal life. So I would have to get a meeting with him even though I had no business seeing him at all.

I entered his building then took the elevator to the top floor. Right when the doors opened, I came face-to-face with three secretaries all sitting behind a white desk. It was extremely quiet, and it seemed like music should play overhead. A white wall was behind them, blocking the rest of the office from view.

A pretty blonde addressed me. "How can I help you?"

"Hello." I walked up to the desk. "I was wondering if Mr. Remington is available for about five minutes?"

Her fake smile immediately turned into a catty look. "Do you have an appointment?"

"Well, no—"

"Then he doesn't have five minutes. He doesn't have any time. He's very busy, far busier than you could possibly imagine. So, if you think—"

This bitch was annoying. "Take a breath, honey." I walked around the desk and helped myself to the back, finding him in a large office completely surrounded by glass walls. He had a perfect view of the city and the park right through his window. Just his office alone was as big as my apartment—and I paid a fortune for it.

"You can't do that!" The blond secretary chased after me and grabbed me by the wrist. "I will call security—"

I twisted out of her grasp. "Touch me like that again, and see what happens."

She slowly lowered her hand, her eyes fuming. She stomped her foot then rushed back to the desk to call security.

When I turned back to his office, his eyes were on me. Brown like hot coffee and deep like the sea, they were so eye-catching, they were impossible to ignore. He stayed in his seat as he watched me, his suit fitting his broad shoulders as well as it did in pictures.

I walked past the sitting area then opened the door to his office.

He stared at me—full of hostility.

"I'm sorry—"

"Don't apologize while you do something wrong. It seems insincere."

I let the door shut behind me, caught off guard by the deepness in his voice. His thick body was tight with rage, and he didn't hide his annoyance at my presence. His hair was a little longer than it was in the pictures, and the subtle beard around his jaw didn't hide how chiseled his appearance was. Then he rose to his feet, buttoning the front of his suit as he moved.

The guy gave me chills.

He was threatening, beautiful, and terrifying.

"What do you want?" He slid his hands into his pockets. "I have someone meeting me in five minutes."

"That's ironic. Five minutes is all I need." I slowly stepped toward his desk, my heels tapping against the hardwood floor of his office.

"Ironic. I'm not amused."

I carried the folder in my hands and set it on his

desk, wondering if this had all been a huge mistake. "I don't know how to go about this—"

"You usually make an appointment with one of my secretaries first."

I grew timid as he continued to bark at me, and I wondered if I could let him fuck me for money. Was he this much of an asshole all the time? I was the one who barged into his office without permission. "I'll be straight with you. I heard you…pay women for their V-cards. A friend of mine told me."

His expression was just as cold as ever, not altering in the slightest way.

"And well…I'm interested…I guess."

"Max handles all of that for me."

"Who's Max?"

He grabbed a business card from one of his drawers and set it at the edge of his desk. "Contact him. He'll take care of you."

I took the card in my hands and saw Max's name and number written on it. He didn't have a last name. There was no company logo. "Alright…"

He returned to his seat and looked at his computer again, like I hadn't disturbed him in the first place. "Get out of my office. And don't come back."

I grabbed the folder I'd placed on his desk and slowly retreated. "Sorry…"

"What did I say about empty apologies?" He kept looking at his computer, so bored with me, he wouldn't even look at me. There was a decanter of scotch on his desk, a picture frame, and a gray MacBook Air.

I stilled in the doorway. "Right." I finally stepped out

and walked away, relieved our interaction was over. I'd never done anything more humiliating in my life, stormed into a stranger's office and basically asked for money in exchange for sex.

Not my finest hour.

———

I CALLED Max when I got to my apartment.

"Max here," he barked into the phone.

"Uh, hi. Slate told me to call you…"

"You spoke to Slate?" he asked in surprise.

"Well, I stopped by his office."

"Do you know him?" He kept firing back with a million questions.

"No. I was trying to find information about…what he likes to spend his money on. He gave me your card and told me to call you."

"So you barged into his office and asked him to take your virginity?" he asked incredulously.

"Well…not in those words."

"That must have pissed him off. His office is a place for business—not his kinks."

"Yeah…I realize that now." I sat on the couch and drank my wine, the cheap kind that cost five bucks for a whole box. "Anyway, now that I have you on the phone, what do I need to know?"

"You don't need to know anything. Text me a picture of yourself along with your name. If Slate approves, I'll contact you."

"Approves?" Was I livestock in a fair contest?

"Yes. He doesn't take just anyone, and I'm guessing he may not be inclined to take you after you barged into his office this afternoon."

"His secretary was a bitch, alright?"

"The blonde one?" he asked.

"Yep."

"I know exactly who you're talking about," he said with a chuckle. "So send me a picture. If he likes what he sees, I'll arrange a dinner."

"Dinner?" Why did we need to have dinner?

"Mr. Remington likes to make sure there's chemistry first."

"Wow, he really is picky."

"You have no idea, sweetheart."

"It doesn't need to be a nude picture, right?"

"It doesn't hurt." He hung up.

3

Slate

A WOMAN HAD NEVER BARGED INTO MY OFFICE like that.

And looked so lost.

She had no idea what she was doing, had no idea how this process worked, and she looked like a deer in headlights.

But she was stunning.

Her tight pencil skirt showed her exceptionally narrow waist, and her long legs were tanned, like she jogged in the park on Saturday afternoons. She had a slim waist and generous tits. She wasn't a C cup, but her tits were proportionally big compared to her waistline. She had soft shoulders, a pretty collarbone, and deep brunette hair.

Perfect ten.

I might have negotiated with her on the spot if she hadn't pissed me off.

She'd barged in there like she could do whatever she

wanted, and I didn't like an arrogant woman. I was already an insanely arrogant man. There wasn't room for two of us.

I was in my penthouse when Max called me. "So, a crazy one stopped by your office?"

I set the phone on the sound system so I could hear him throughout the living room. I headed to the bar to make myself a drink. After working all day and hitting the gym, I was in my sweatpants, and all I wanted was a glass of booze in my hand. "She wasn't crazy. Just stupid."

"Same thing if you ask me. I just sent you her picture. She's not nude, so maybe she doesn't want the gig that bad."

I added a few ice cubes then walked back to my phone. I opened the message and clicked on the picture. It was a selfie she took of herself, and since she wore the same outfit she had on earlier, she must have snapped it the second she got home. "Or because I've already seen her in person."

"She can't expect you to remember."

I definitely remembered.

"So, what's your take?"

I sat on the couch and finally took a drink, letting the liquid drip down my throat. If someone else stormed into my office like that, they would forfeit their chance. But she was too beautiful for me to reject. I bedded beautiful women all the time, and my obsession had become a sickness. I loved to watch them cry, loved to watch them struggle to take my big dick. Not only did I break them in, but I ruined all other men for them. "I'll have dinner with her."

"Really?" he asked in surprise. "I thought you were going to say no."

"We'll have dinner first and see what happens." I put my feet on the coffee table then turned on the TV. My penthouse was the entire top floor of my building, so I had 7,000 square feet to myself. It could get quiet sometimes, but I loved the quiet. I loved the solitude. "Arrange it."

"Whatever you say, boss."

4

Monroe

I was meeting Slate at a fancy place, so I wore a cocktail dress I'd bought five years ago. Thankfully, I'd stayed the same size because I couldn't afford enough food to make me gain weight. My heels were also old, but after a good shine, they looked as good as new. I put some cheap earrings in my lobes, grabbed my clutch, and then left the apartment.

I was so nervous.

I wouldn't be sleeping with him tonight. It was just a meeting, not any different from a job interview.

Except, in this case, I was applying to be fucked.

For the first time.

After the awkward conversation in his office, I was surprised he even agreed to dinner with me. Most women probably sent provocative photos of themselves in white panties, but I refused to do that. He'd already seen me in person, so a dirty pic wouldn't make a difference.

After walking a few blocks, I arrived at the restaurant. It was a French bistro with a European menu. It was the kind of place I would love to go to, but it simply didn't work with my budget. That was my problem for the evening. I wanted to pay for my meal, but frankly, I couldn't afford it.

How pathetic was that?

If I spent my last twenty bucks, I wouldn't have a penny until I got paid on Monday. My card would probably get rejected anyway, and that would be even more embarrassing. So hopefully, he would offer to pay and save me the humiliation.

I didn't see him in the lobby so I stepped up to the podium. "I'm meeting Slate Remington—"

"Yes, this way." She stepped around the podium then walked with me through the restaurant. The floor was made of gold tile, the tables were black, and a grand piano was in the center of the room, where a woman played serene music. The hostess took me to a different section of the restaurant, a quieter place where the tables were spread out much farther. It seemed to be a VIP section where the rich and famous could let their hair down.

When I rounded the corner, I saw him sitting in a private booth against the wall. He'd ditched his suit and wore a black t-shirt with dark jeans. The dress code requested something dressier, but he clearly didn't think that applied to him.

He lifted his gaze to look at me, and those chocolate-colored eyes looked deep into my soul. He didn't smile politely or rise to greet me. Stone-cold and hostile, he stared at me like he wished he were somewhere else.

This should be fun.

I slid into the booth across from him, crossed my legs, and pretended I wasn't intimidated by him. I should have known it wouldn't be so easy as sleeping with a beautiful man and getting paid for it. I should have known there would be a catch, a contingency.

And that contingency was that he was an asshole.

He already had a drink on the table, rum and Coke. He stared at me without making conversation, like the never-ending silence didn't bother him at all. He was so confident that the most awkward situation in the world wouldn't unnerve him.

It unnerved me, but I refused to show it. "So you're this unpleasant all the time? Whether you're in your office or not?" I wanted this man to sleep with me, so being a smartass was probably stupid, but I couldn't change my personality. Maybe I wanted the money, but he was also getting something valuable in return.

"Always." He grabbed his glass and took a long drink.

"That's great…" I looked at the menu and didn't struggle to find something I wanted. After all, I was starving, and the cramping of my stomach constantly reminded me of that. I decided on the steak, something that would last me a few days.

When the waitress arrived, Slate ordered for me. "She'll have a rum and Coke as well." He turned to me. "Are you ready to order?"

"Do I get a choice?" I snapped, not caring that the

waitress witnessed the exchange. "Actually, I'll have a glass of red wine. It'll go well with the steak—medium rare." I handed over my menu.

Slate handed his over as well. "I'll have the same—minus the wine."

She walked away and left us alone.

He leaned back and gently drummed his fingers on the table.

"So…you invite me to dinner but don't engage in conversation?"

"The purpose of dinner is to see if there's chemistry. And I don't need to talk to you to figure that out." He drank from his glass again.

"And have you figured it out?"

"I think so."

I waited for an answer.

He clearly had no intention of giving it to me. "How old are you?"

"You never ask a woman that question."

"I'm asking it anyway." His muscular arms stretched the sleeves of his t-shirt. Every group of muscle was distinct and separate, the cords running all the way down to his hands. His skin was tanned, like he spent time outside, probably on a yacht or something. Last time I saw him, he had a bit of a beard, but he must have shaved before our date.

"Twenty-three."

His brown eyes slightly narrowed. "That's a little old to be a virgin."

"Are you suggesting I'm lying?"

"No. I'll know if you're lying soon enough." He

brought the glass to his lips and took another drink, downing the contents like water rather than hard alcohol. "I fucked a girl for the first time when I was fifteen—that's almost a decade before you."

"It's not a race."

"But I'm curious why you've been waiting so long. It's something you should enjoy as much as you can."

"It just didn't work out."

"Work out?" he asked. "You're a gorgeous woman. You could have made it work out any night of the week. So why didn't you?"

"Does it matter?"

"It does to me."

No one ever asked me these kinds of questions because they were intimate and rude. But Slate Remington had no problem asking—because he was paying for it. "I was planning on sleeping with my prom date in high school, but he ended up hooking up with someone else by the end of the night. In college, I found a steady boyfriend, but I wanted to take things slow. He got frustrated and started screwing someone else. I was about to sleep with him when I found out…and then it never happened. After that, I was kinda over men for a while."

"Because you're making it a bigger deal than it needs to be. Sex is just sex. People read too much into it."

"Maybe you're right…"

"I am right." He finished his glass then waved to the waitress to bring him another. "I'm always right."

"Sometimes, you're right. But you're always arrogant."

The waitress switched out the glasses and walked away.

"So, I hear they call you the Cherry Popper."

He gave a slight bow. "At your service."

"You really call yourself that?"

He shrugged. "The name fits."

"You've been doing this for a long time?"

"Five years and counting."

He'd been fucking virgins for money for five years? "Why?"

"Why what?"

"Why would you pay a lot of money to fuck virgins?"

He cocked his head slightly. "Maybe it's a lot of money to you, but it's pennies to me. And I'm the one who should be asking the questions here."

"I signed the NDA Max sent over, so I'm harmless." If I told anyone about this, he would sue me for three times what he would pay me. It would put me further into debt and really ruin my life.

"I just prefer virgins."

"Because…?"

He raised an eyebrow. "I know you're inexperienced, but think about it. A woman's first time is sexy. She'll never be tighter than she is in that moment. She'll have to stretch for me as I ruin her. She'll cry because it hurts. But I'll still make her come, give her a good experience, rather than the nightmare she would receive from some other guy. A woman's first time is almost always shitty."

Cherry Popper

I'd been trying to lose my V-card for a while, but I always ended up in a crappy situation. If I had slept with either of those guys, it probably would have been a bad memory. "So you date women and fuck virgins in between?"

He wrapped his hand around his glass, his fingers feeling the condensation. "No. I *only* fuck virgins."

It took me a minute to understand what he meant. "Exclusively?"

"Yes."

"And then it's on to the next one?"

"Yes."

This guy was a bigger asshole than I realized.

"And that's the only kind of woman I'll ever fuck for the rest of my life."

Only a truly arrogant son of a bitch would live his life that way.

"They're clean. They're tight. And they're vulnerable."

I shook my head in disgust. "Wow…you're such an ass."

"You're the one who asked. You're the one who wants to be like the rest of them."

"Not *want*," I corrected. "I just have to."

He took a long drink as he kept his eyes on me, his masculine throat tightening and shifting as he got the liquor into his stomach. "Some of the women I fuck don't ask for money. Some of them just want me to pop their cherry."

"Why?" I asked, not having a clue why someone would do that.

"Because I'm good at it. I can make a woman's first time be their best time."

I had a feeling that wouldn't be the case for me. "You just said you enjoy it when they cry."

"Because my dick is so big that it hurts. But they push past that and start to enjoy it."

I wondered how big his dick was. I would ask, but I'd probably find out soon enough.

"Why do you need the money so badly? You obviously wouldn't do this unless you had no other choice."

I grabbed my wine and finally took a drink, savoring the luxurious smoothness on my tongue. It was so much better than the boxed wine I had at home. I wanted to enjoy it as much as possible. "I have a shit-ton of student loans. I made a lot of mistakes I wish I could take back."

"How is getting an education a mistake?"

"Because I paid too much for it. I went to UCLA when I should have gone to a cheaper school. I got my masters at NYU immediately after, when I should have skipped the masters altogether. Now I'm nearly $200,000 in debt…because I was too young and naïve to know better."

"Where do you work now?"

"I'm a marketing executive at Cutie Clothes. It's a good job and pays well, but the cost of living is so high and my loans are so expensive that I can barely afford to live. I would have been better off not getting an education and just finding a job in Connecticut."

"Why Connecticut?"

"That's where I'm originally from," I explained. "And my student loans aren't even my biggest problem."

He abandoned his drink and leaned forward, his muscular arms on the table. When he came closer to me, his masculine cheekbones and chiseled jawline were even more noticeable. The moody lighting of the restaurant played with his features well. But then again, he was so handsome, he looked good in any light. "What's your biggest problem?"

"I have a huge medical bill that I'll be paying off for the rest of my life."

It was the first time he dropped his arrogance and actually looked like a human being. The hostility in his eyes died away, and now he looked at me like I'd said something that actually affected him. "Are you alright?"

"It wasn't for me. My mother had cervical cancer, and there was this new cancer cure that had been introduced that year. It was still in the trial phase, but it had great statistics, so I wanted to give it a try. I knew it might not work, but I refused to give up. My mother was under the impression it was much cheaper than it really was… Otherwise, she wouldn't have done it."

His eyes softened further. "Was?"

I shook my head. "You know the ending…"

"I'm sorry." It seemed like he meant it, even though he'd just spoken about fucking virgins and making them cry.

"She passed away a year ago. Her insurance covered most of her treatments, but that last trial is under my name."

"How much was it?"

"You don't want to know…"

"Tell me," he said quietly.

"Four hundred and fifty…"

"Thousand?" he asked incredulously.

I nodded. "I don't regret it. She's my mother… I had to do everything to save her."

He sighed as he looked down into his drink. "That's rough, Monroe."

"Yeah…it hasn't been easy." I had over $600,000 in debt, and I didn't even own a house or a car. I'd spend my life paying that back, and as a result, I would never be able to afford to buy myself anything.

"What about your father?"

"He passed away about ten years ago. Veteran."

"Did he pass away in the line of duty?"

"Yes. He was a medic."

"I'm sorry…again."

I drank my wine. "Thanks."

"But his service should be able to help with your school somehow."

"It did," I said with a nod. "I used his GI bill to fund some of my undergrad work. But it only covers so much. It's unfortunate that my parents did their best to give me a better life, but I got crushed by the system. Even without my mother's medical treatment, I would still be struggling. The American dream isn't what it used to be."

Slate didn't have anything to say to that. He was a multimillionaire, probably a billionaire. He didn't know what it meant to struggle. He probably didn't go to college because he didn't need to. He probably inherited all of his opportunities. "Now I understand why you hunted me down so adamantly."

"I didn't hunt you down… I just didn't know where to go. I'm not even sure how I would have found Max if you hadn't given me his card."

"It's an underground thing. Technically, what I do is illegal, even though the cops wouldn't do shit if they found out."

Because he had enough money to make them go away. "So, you're just going to keep doing this for the rest of your life? When you're forty? Fifty?"

"Pretty much."

"I'm guessing you don't date? Have girlfriends?"

"Never." He brought his glass to his lips. "Monogamy has never interested me. Why have mediocre sex with an awesome person, when I can have amazing sex every night with a different person? Because every time really is the first time—at least for her."

"That seems kinda sad to me."

"You're a twenty-three-year-old virgin. You don't know any better. But once you have it…you'll see what I mean. You'll be out on the town every weekend looking for a good lay because you'll want more. But you'll never find it…because I'm the best."

"I'm sure the man I marry will be the best."

"There it is again…that naïve optimism. When you start experimenting with other men, you'll realize there's no such thing as Prince Charming. Men are all dogs that only care about themselves. Trust me on that."

I gave him the same sad look he just gave me. He might be a rich and powerful man who seemed to have everything, but below that projection, there was just a broken soul underneath. Why else would he be constantly angry? Why else would he drink liquor like water? Why else would he pay money to take a woman's most intimate experience? "Not all men are like you, Slate."

5

Slate

She ate everything on her plate, the entire eight-ounce steak, along with the potatoes and greens. She didn't shovel the food into her mouth like she was starving. She took her time, ate slowly, but instead of filling up quickly, her appetite never seemed to end. Once her plate was clean, she drank her wine.

Even I could only eat half. "Hungry?"

"I skipped lunch today."

Monroe was different from the other women who approached me. I'd noticed it the second I laid eyes on her, when she stepped into my office despite the promise of death written on my face. She blasted through my secretaries like they were no hindrance at all. Then she basically asked me to take her virginity right in the middle of my office, while making it clear she despised herself for doing it.

Now that I knew about her debt, it all made sense.

She really didn't have a choice.

As we sat across from each other at dinner, it was clear she thought very little of me. She wasn't impressed by my money, even though she had none, and while she was attracted to my looks, she certainly wasn't attracted to anything that popped out of my mouth. She was very innocent, not just because of her purity, but because of her outlook on life. After having no real experience with men, she thought there were good guys out there.

No such thing.

All men wanted to be pigs. All men wanted to be rich, powerful, and fuck an endless line of beautiful women. But that was a fantasy they could never achieve, so they settled for what they could get—one woman who would tolerate them. She mistakenly referred to men like that as Prince Charming.

The poor girl had a lot to learn about the real world.

She signed her name on a bill she could never repay, just for the slight chance her mother might survive. No one else would have done that because they had more sensibility. She was too optimistic.

And that was why she was in this situation in the first place.

I held my glass as I stared at her, watched the lipstick marks stick to her glass in several places. She had deep brown hair, fair skin the color of snow, and lips so red they resembled blood. The occasional freckle on her cheek contrasted against her pure skin, the only seeming imperfection on a beautiful face. With that stunning frame and even more stunning looks, she could have led a much different life. All she needed was to use that confidence to her advantage, and she could have paved the streets in gold. She could have pursued modeling or acting. She could have easily been a top-billed porn star. Instead, she focused on the books like a nerd for an office job.

What a shame.

Dinners like these were used to gauge my interest in the woman. I didn't just fuck anyone. I needed to feel chemistry, to feel some sort of passion. I got so many offers that I rejected most of them. So women were always on their best behavior, saying what I wanted to hear in the hope they would be chosen.

Monroe acted like she didn't want to be chosen at all.

The best way for me to determine my attraction was by the tightness in my jeans. If I felt myself go hard during the meal because of the way she drank from her glass or licked her lips, I knew she was a suitable lay.

And Monroe kept me hard through almost the entire dinner.

When she pulled her hair over one shoulder and revealed her stunning neck, I saw the same breathtaking skin, the softness my lips wanted to caress. She had a graceful neck, slender and long. Her black dress revealed a bit of her collarbone, and that was nice too. I wanted to give it a slight nibble as I kissed her.

She was taller than the average woman, which was something else I liked. Most women were barely over five feet, but this woman had to be at least five six. She wasn't close to my height, but at least she was compatible. Women always assumed tall men wanted short women. Not me.

Her tits were my favorite feature. She was busty for her size, fuller in her chest than she should be. For a woman with a tiny waist and a low body weight, her boobs were unnaturally big. Since she was broke, I knew they were real.

I'd never cared for fake tits.

My cock thickened a little more in my jeans when I imagined her underneath me, her tight pussy fighting my intrusion. Once I got my length inside, I would take it easy on her for the first minute, give her a chance to get used to it. Then I would fuck her harder, break her in, and enjoy her cunt to the fullest. It always turned me on when they cried underneath me, and I hoped she did the same, but I suspected she was too proud to do that.

"What?" She returned her glass to the table and licked her lips.

"I didn't say anything."

"I know. But you're staring at me."

"And I'll keep staring." My glass was empty, and my meal was finished. Now, all that was left was thinking about her on her back, her tits in my face.

"What are you thinking about? Must be something important to wear an expression like that."

"Fucking you," I blurted. "That's what I was thinking about."

She held my gaze without fear, but it was clear my bluntness unnerved her.

The waitress collected the plates and left the tab behind.

She eyed it before she looked at me. "I'd like to offer

to pay for my meal. You know, since this isn't a date. But—"

"No." I pulled out a wad of cash from my wallet and slipped it inside. She was in financial crisis, and there was no way in hell I was letting her pay for a hundred-dollar meal. "That's not how this works."

"Well…thank you."

"You're welcome."

She finished her wine and left the empty glass on the table. "So, now what?"

"Ordinarily, we would say goodnight, and Max would let you know if I'm interested."

"So you actually reject women?" she asked incredulously.

"All the time."

She continued to wear her surprised expression. "But isn't that exactly what you want? Virgin after virgin?"

"Sometimes, I'm not attracted to them. Sometimes, there's no chemistry. And when you have a high volume of submissions, you can't get through everyone. You have to choose."

"That many women actually come to you?"

"Why does that surprise you?"

"Uh, because it's degrading…?"

I shrugged. "You get paid well to sleep with a handsome man. It's not like I'm into some weird shit like BDSM."

"I think this still constitutes weird shit. And handsome man?" she asked. "You're really going to call yourself that?"

"Are you saying I'm not?" I countered.

She didn't give an answer. "Just think it's arrogant…"

"I'm very arrogant, so it fits."

"So I go home and just sit by the phone?"

"No. I already have an answer for you." She ran her mouth constantly and spoke her mind, and I found that oddly refreshing. Women were determined to be quiet and well-behaved, like that was what men wanted. But when Monroe gave her opinions, it reminded me of the suits I worked with on a daily basis. They were aggressive when they spoke their mind—and they made shit happen.

"And what is that answer?"

If only she could see my dick. "Are you free tomorrow night?"

6

Monroe

I couldn't believe I was doing this.

The package arrived at my door. Inside was a key to room 943 along with white lingerie in my size. I was instructed to wear it under my clothes, and once I was inside the room, I was supposed to lie on the bed in just the lingerie.

Then he would appear.

I looked at myself in the mirror, seeing the endless strings of the lingerie piece. The bra was so thin, my tits were perfectly visible, and the thong below was made of the same material. So I wore something, but I also wore nothing at all. I shaved everything that morning and submitted all my tests to Max—and also got the shot in my arm for birth control.

Because Slate wouldn't wear a condom.

Not only was I giving myself to this man—I was letting him come inside me.

It felt a million times dirtier.

I pulled my black dress over my head to hide my lingerie from view, and I felt the guilt consume me. My mother would be so disappointed in me if she knew what I was doing. Even if I had a one-night stand with some random guy just to get it over with, that would be fine—because it was my choice. But I was only doing this for the money—and that kinda made me a whore.

But I didn't have any other choice. That money would make my life so much easier.

I grabbed my purse and walked out the door, breathing hard because I knew what was about to happen. I couldn't take a cab because I couldn't afford it, so I walked seventeen blocks until I reached his hotel. It was across the street from the park. It was enormous, glamorous, and fancy.

I stared at the double doors for a moment before I walked inside.

A weight settled on my shoulders, and the dread kicked in. It didn't matter that I'd had an extra day to think about it since we'd had to wait for the shot to take effect; I was still apprehensive. I headed to the elevator doors and hit the button with a shaky hand. It seemed like I was marching to my doom rather than to a passionate night of lovemaking. It didn't matter that Slate Remington was one of the most handsome men I'd ever seen.

This just felt wrong.

I rode the elevator to my floor then located the room where I was supposed to meet him. I knew he didn't live in his hotel, but he probably didn't want to bring random women back to his residence.

Cherry Popper

I slipped the card into the door, and then it unlocked.

I stepped inside the large suite, coming into a living room with a set of couches, a large TV, and a bar. The floor-to-ceiling windows revealed the lights of the city as they showcased Central Park. "Slate?" I stepped farther into the room and placed my purse on the dining table.

There was no answer.

I turned to the left and spotted the large king-size bed against the wall. The comforter was dark red, along with the pillows. On the wall were portraits of cherries. I stared at the spot and realized this was the exact place all the women before me had lost their virtues. I would be one of many. He probably wouldn't even remember this night in a few years.

I began to loathe myself for what I was doing. I was even tempted to walk out and call the whole thing off. But when I walked back to get my purse, I noticed the check sitting there. It was addressed to me—and it was for $100,000.

Seeing the money with my own eyes reminded me why I was here. It reminded me that thirty minutes of my life would fix a lot of my problems. All I had to do was lie there and wait for him to finish. It might hurt, but it couldn't be the worst pain in the world. I might bleed, but at least I would ruin his sheets and not mine. Then I could go out and start dating without having to carry around my V-card anymore.

I stared at the check a moment longer before I pulled my dress over my head. I slipped off my heels and left them on the floor. Now I stood in the white ensemble, an untouched virgin waiting to be taken by an arrogant playboy.

I moved back to the bed and took a seat, waiting for him as instructed.

He walked inside several minutes later, wearing a suit and tie like he'd just left the office. He came into my line of sight as he took off his clothes. First came the jacket and then his tie. He set it on the back of the chair before he unbuttoned his shirt and stripped it away.

His body was hard like his arms. He was over six feet of pure muscle, of powerful striations in between the sections of strength. He had a perfect back that rippled every time he moved, and his tanned skin made his muscles even sexier.

He really was a beautiful man.

He moved to his slacks next and pushed them down until he was just in his boxers.

"Is this where you always—"

He turned to me, ferocity in his gaze. "No talking."

I shut my mouth, not in obedience, but shock.

He walked to the edge of the bed and looked down at me, an appreciative look in his eyes. His gaze wandered over my body in approval as his cock twitched in his shorts. The outline was noticeable, and it only got bigger. Soon he poked out from underneath the fabric, his thick head impressive.

He wasn't kidding. He did have a big dick.

"Ever had a cock in your mouth?" He lowered his shorts slowly, revealing every inch of his monstrous length.

"I thought I wasn't supposed to talk?" I tried not to

stare at his dick too much. I was aroused by it but also terrified of it. There was no way it would fit inside me. No wonder why the other women cried. I'd cry too.

His eyes darkened in irritation. "Answer the question."

"Yes. I've sucked dick before. I'm a virgin—not a freak."

"Then get to it." His hand moved to my neck, and he pulled me toward him instantly, not even allowing me to make the decision on my own.

I jerked back. "You aren't even going to kiss me first?"

His hand stayed on my neck, his fingers tightening in annoyance. "All I want to do is fuck that mouth. So, open wide, and don't choke." He pulled me to him again.

This time, I turned my face away and stood up. "You're such an asshole, I can't believe it."

"I'm an asshole? Trust me, you're going to want me to be as wet as possible before I fuck you. And this isn't going to be a fairy tale. You've sold your virginity to me, and I will take it however I chose. Now get on your fucking knees and suck my dick." He stepped toward me, his hostility burning with power. He was tall, muscular, and so authoritative he could lead an army into battle.

I needed that money so badly, but I didn't want this night to happen. I didn't want to live with the shame of getting on my knees for an asshole like him. How would I be able to look my husband in the eye knowing what I did? That I'd allowed a man to disrespect me just for money? That's when I knew I couldn't go through with it. "I've changed my mind." I stepped around him and headed to the dining table where my dress sat. The check was there, but this time, I couldn't let it entice me.

He came after me, his dick still hard despite his ferocity. He grabbed me by the arm and forced me to turn around.

"I said no—"

He cupped my face and brought his lips to mine. He kissed me, but not aggressively like I expected. It was soft, purposeful, and so slow, it seemed like he was a different man. His fingers moved into my hair, and he fisted it gently, cradling my head rather than yanking on it.

The kiss was so nice I forgot about my stampede. It was soft, the way a woman always wanted to be kissed by a lover. I melted instantly at his touch, forgetting the cruel way he'd just bossed me around a second ago.

His other arm hooked around my waist, and he pulled me tight against his body, letting me feel his dick right against my stomach. He squeezed me as he continued the kiss, giving me his tongue and his warm breaths.

My hands touched his chest for the first time, and I felt how strong he was. Like he was a solid wall, I felt his hardness, felt his power. My mouth kept moving with his as I sensed the chemistry he mentioned before, the passion between two people innately attracted to one another. When words flew out of his mouth, he was unbearable. But when there was silence, he really was beautiful.

He slowly guided me back to the bed, his kiss never stopping as he pressed the backs of my knees against the mattress. He ended the kiss and slowly guided me into a sitting position, back to where I'd been just a second before. One hand grabbed his length, while the other cupped my face. "Open, sweetheart."

Now that his kiss had sedated my rage, I opened my mouth and flattened my tongue.

He slowly guided himself inside and moaned when he felt my wet warmth. His hand moved to the back of my head to support me as he started to thrust. He didn't even give me an opportunity to give him a blow job. He just fucked my mouth like he said he would, slamming deep inside me until I could barely breathe.

He stared at me with a focused look on his face, his eyes concentrating and his jaw clenched tight. He shoved his cock as deep as he could go, hitting the back of my throat hard with every thrust. Most of his length couldn't even fit, but that didn't stop him from trying.

I gripped his thighs and tried to lean back so I wouldn't have to take so much of his length, but his hand forced me into position.

He turned rough again, treating my throat like an experienced pussy.

That was when I pulled my mouth away.

He didn't try to do it again. "On the bed."

I scooted back until my head hit the pillow. My mouth was full of saliva now, and his taste was still on my tongue.

He moved over me and yanked my thong off my

body. He didn't bother with the top before he positioned himself between my legs and prepared to fuck me.

It wasn't slow. It wasn't romantic. It wasn't what I envisioned my first time to be.

But I just had to lie there for thirty minutes until he was done.

That was nothing.

I could do that.

But when he pressed his fat head against my entrance, I knew I couldn't do it. I couldn't live with this memory. I would just have to find three roommates and live in a shithole to survive. It was better than giving up like this. "No…get off me."

He stayed still, like he couldn't believe what I'd just said.

"I said, get off me."

He stayed put, and for a second, it seemed like he might do it anyway. But then he rolled off me.

I left my thong on the ground and moved to the dining room to fetch my dress. I pulled it over my body quickly, slipped on my heels, and then grabbed my purse. I was ashamed of myself for coming here at all, for letting him fuck my throat like it was a toy.

"Monroe—"

"I know fairy tales don't exist." I turned around to face him. "But I don't want this to be my first time. I don't want this memory. Maybe sex is meaningless, but I don't want my first time to be meaningless. I need that money, but I need my self-respect more. I'm sorry for wasting your time—but I just can't do it." I walked out and left the check behind. When I got to the door, I expected him to try to talk me out of it. But he didn't. He let me go. I shut the door behind me, and when I got to the elevator, I finally released the breath I was holding.

The elevator took me to the lobby—took me to freedom.

7

Slate

My penthouse was too big for one person, but I liked it because it made me feel alone.

Made me feel alone in a city as big as Manhattan.

My floor was high enough that I could barely hear the sirens of the police cars. Only an occasional chopper passed near my window, and even then, I could barely hear the rotor blades. For being a big player in the hospitality industry, I really disliked people.

Monroe turned down my money and left the hotel room without looking back. Her throat felt nice around my dick, and that kiss was exquisite. I didn't kiss women very often, only if they made the move first, and even then, I didn't enjoy it much.

But I liked kissing Monroe.

She had the softest lips, the perfect amount of hesitation and determination. Her hands moved to her chest as she enjoyed me, as she immediately forgot how much she hated me. The lust beat out her logic, and she came back to the bed with hungry hands.

But when the good stuff was about to start, she bailed.

Her dislike outweighed her need for money.

She despised me that much.

I understood I was an asshole. I understood I was unbearable at times. But it didn't seem like the other women cared that much.

But she definitely cared.

It was more than she could handle.

I WAS SITTING in my office when Max walked inside. "I've got some new takers." He placed the folder on the table. "They all check out."

I didn't pick up the folder. Instead, I stared at my computer screen like he wasn't even there.

"How did it go with Monroe? She seems feisty."

"Very," I answered. "But it didn't go. She bailed."

"Really?" he asked. "She's more than $600,000 in debt, but she left?"

I nodded. "She's not my biggest fan."

"Well, not many people are," he said with a grin. "So, let me know which of my girls you like. They're all over twenty-one—as you requested."

If they weren't legal to drink, then they were too young for me. "I'll get back to you."

Max slid his hands into his pockets as he stood at my desk. "Everything alright, sir?"

"She's the first woman to walk out on me." I turned in my chair to face him, the rejection starting to sting. She'd turned down me and the cash because she didn't see a reason to stay. I shouldn't care, but I did.

"She's different. Don't worry about her."

"Maybe that's why I like her…because she's different."

"Do you want me to reach out to her again? See if I can change her mind?"

I wouldn't send my dog to fetch her. Not for something like this. "No. I'll take care of it."

I HAD HER INFORMATION, so finding her address was simple enough. She lived on the opposite side of town from my penthouse, so she had to take two different subway routes just to make it to work. But I'm sure her location was based on what she could afford—which wasn't much.

The other women didn't come to me because they were in extreme debt. Most of them just wanted the cash to buy a new car or put a down payment on an apartment. Some of them just wanted to go on a trip of a lifetime. For them, it wasn't a matter of survival. But for Monroe, it certainly was. She'd managed to dig herself into a black hole, something even light couldn't escape from. She had no options, but she was still too proud to give herself away.

I admired it.

Even though it annoyed me.

I showed up at her apartment at close to seven in the evening. I knew she got off work at five and then rode the subway for almost an hour before she made it home. My guy told me she lived alone, so that made this easier.

I knocked on her door and stepped back so she could see my face through the peephole.

A few locks turned, and then she opened the door.

She stared at me in horror, like I was the very last person she ever wanted to see. Her hair was straight around her shoulders, and she wore a maroon dress with a black belt around her waist. Her shoes were gone because she'd probably kicked them off the second she got off work. Her hand gripped the door as she studied me, trying to decide if I was real or this was just a nightmare.

I was in my suit and tie because I didn't bother changing at my penthouse before I came over here. I'd replayed our last interaction in my mind so many times that it was all I could think about. Stopping to change would have taken too much time, not when I was desperate to see her face-to-face. "Can I come inside? Or are you always this rude?"

Her shocked expression quickly hardened into an offended one. "Not as rude as you."

I crossed the threshold and invited myself inside. I moved my body into her apartment, forcing her to step back and give me more space to enter her living room. I didn't have high expectations for her living situation, so I wasn't surprised to see the single couch and small table comprise her living room, along with a small TV. Her kitchen was only a few feet wide, there wasn't a dining table, and there was a door that connected to her bedroom. It had to be a few hundred square feet at the most.

I could hear the sirens audibly, along with her neighbors fighting next door. It sounded like a married couple with a crying baby. The more they fought, the harder the baby cried. The walls seemed to be paper-thin.

"How can I help you?" She shut the door behind her and held as much pride as she could, considering the yelling next door kept increasing in volume. "I would offer you a drink, but I only have water—on tap."

"No thanks." I felt like an asshole standing there in a suit that cost me $10,000. It was probably what she paid in taxes over the course of a year.

She crossed her arms over her chest and looked visibly uncomfortable, like having me in her space made her stomach churn. She was probably thinking about that night in detail, from the way I kissed her softly then fucked her throat.

I knew I was thinking about it.

"Why are you here, Slate?" she asked. "If you're mad at me because of the other night, I won't apologize for it."

"I didn't expect you to." She'd wasted my time when another woman wouldn't. I had a dozen girls who would have killed to take her place. I could have spent the evening fucking them instead of watching her tease me then storm off.

"Then what do you want? To pay you back for the dinner we had the other night?"

My eyebrows immediately furrowed at the suggestion. I might be an asshole, but I wasn't that petty. "No."

"To yell at me for leaving?"

"No."

She crossed her arms over her waist and glanced at my chest, like direct eye contact was too intimate. Her dress fit her snugly around the waist, her petite frame noticeable in the tight clothing. She had a perfect hourglass frame, which was gorgeous in the lingerie ensemble she'd worn that night. But she could wear a garbage bag and still steal focus. "Then why are you here?"

"To change your mind." My hands rested in the pockets of my slacks, and I felt my attraction to her grow. No one else could interest me enough to hunt them down like this. There were plenty of other women to take her slot, beautiful women who looked forward to giving themselves to me. I didn't need to waste my time here, but I'd been thinking about her since the moment she walked out on me. I'd jerked off onto her panties because I was so hard up.

She stiffened noticeably, as if the suggestion was unwelcome. "I thought I could do it, but I can't."

"Yes, you can."

"Then let me rephrase it. I don't want to." The more she resisted me, the more beautiful she became. Her naïve morals were a sharp intake of fresh air. Nobody cared about anything anymore, but she preserved her innocence like it meant something.

I stepped toward her, noting the way she didn't step back. My presence slowly came into contact with hers, slowly invaded her personal space. I stopped when our faces were dangerously close, close enough to imply that we were lovers. When she didn't move away, I knew she was still attracted to me, that the kiss we'd shared was one of the pleasant memories she had of me.

She held my gaze with all the courage she could muster, but her slight hint of anxiety told me this was hard for her, that she was intimidated by me like everyone else in the world. But she had the strength to at least fight me rather than submit.

Now that I'd tested the waters and felt how warm they were, my hand slid to her cheek, and I brought our faces close together. That kiss we shared had been on my mind, along with that little white thong she left behind. The kiss had been passionate and slow, the kind of kiss I hadn't shared with a lover in so long. My thumb brushed across her bottom lip before I leaned in and kissed her.

My lips lightly rested against hers, testing her resolve. Which was stronger? Her attraction or her dislike? When she didn't push me away, I felt her lips like last time, gently massaging them with my own. So soft and smooth, they tasted like cherry lip balm. I breathed into her mouth before I kept kissing her, feeling my entire body stiffen and tighten. Warmth flooded my veins just the way alcohol peaked in my blood after a few drinks. Her lips were hesitant, like she knew this was wrong, and the fact that she kept kissing me only made it better. I liked her strength but also her vulnerability. She tried to protect herself from me, but I wasn't the kind of man you could hide from.

Just when my hand moved into her hair and I gripped her waist, she pulled her delicious lips away and bowed her head. I felt her slip from my grasp, her petite waist fleeing my fingertips.

She stepped back and crossed her arms over her chest, like that would somehow keep me away. "If you came here to seduce me, it won't work."

"I just wanted to kiss you. Harmless."

She touched her bottom lip like I'd bit her. "I don't know if I would describe it as harmless."

"You liked it."

"That's exactly the problem." She looked at the ground for a moment before she raised her gaze to meet mine. "You should go."

That kiss only made me want her more, and I wouldn't walk away without a fight. "Let's get some dinner together." Maybe being out of her apartment would make her more comfortable. I didn't come here so I could quickly fuck her on her couch. "And talk."

"I said you won't change my mind."

"Then a dinner won't hurt, right? I'm asking for a meal, not your virginity."

"Actually, you are."

I shrugged. "Well, I'm not asking for it right away. Come on, my treat." For someone like her, a meal out must be a deathblow to her bank account. I'd been wealthy for a long time, so I never had to worry about the cost of anything. I just got what I wanted—even if I didn't really need it. There was no such thing as a budget. "Or we could stand here all night until our knees start to hurt."

My humor seemed to calm her down, because she

smiled. "Alright. But I'm only agreeing because I'm starving."

WE WENT to a deli around the corner because it was the closest thing to walk to. I'd never eaten there or heard of it, but it seemed like she'd visited the place a few times. She knew exactly what she wanted the second she stepped inside. We both ordered our food then carried our trays to a booth in the corner. It was a quiet night, so we pretty much had the entire place to ourselves.

It wasn't the most romantic setting, but maybe that was a good thing.

Like the last time we had a meal together, she ate everything, but she did it slowly, like she was trying to make it last.

"Are you always this hungry?" I asked, only taking a few bites of my sandwich because it was way too many carbs.

"Yes." She opened her bag of chips and popped a few into her mouth. "Do you always eat just a portion of your food?"

"Yes. At least when it's bread."

"I guess that makes sense. You wouldn't have an eight-pack if you ate whatever you wanted all the time."

"You like my eight-pack?" I asked, noting the praise in her voice.

"That's not a fair question. Every woman likes a solid eight-pack."

"Not necessarily. Men can have eight-packs because they have no fat. I have no fat, but I also have a lot of muscle."

She popped another chip into her mouth. "So that's what we're going to talk about tonight? Objectifying your body?"

"Hey, you brought it up."

"Not really."

I rested my arm over the back of the booth as I stared at her, her beautiful face far too stunning for a joint like this. Her apartment annoyed me because she deserved better. But at least she didn't have any roommates.

"Where do you live?"

I raised an eyebrow at the question.

"So you can arrive at my doorstep without warning, but I can't ask where you live?" she asked incredulously.

"I live in Manhattan—close to work."

"So in a penthouse at the top of a skyscraper."

I shrugged. "Maybe. Maybe not."

"I'm going with maybe." She kept eating. "I'm surprised you're here. You said you have a long list of women who would love your attention for the night. I can't imagine why you're here, picking at a sandwich with a woman who can barely tolerate you."

"Barely tolerate? You tolerated me just fine during that kiss."

"That kiss didn't mean anything. It was just a kiss—"

"That you enjoyed."

"So? I enjoyed your dick in my mouth, but that doesn't mean I want to do it again."

The air left my lungs at the casual way she said those words. She clearly possessed the innocence of someone inexperienced, but she also had the confidence of a woman who could do anything.

It took me a few seconds to respond because I couldn't get the image out of my head. If I thought about it too long, I could feel that perfect tongue against the bottom of my shaft. I gripped the back of her head and fucked her mouth like it was a toy rather than part of a person. Despite it being her first time, I certainly wasn't delicate, but I was never delicate. It was my fantasy—not hers. "I'd like to do that again."

"Not gonna happen," she shot back.

Her denial only made me want her more. "I'd like you to reconsider."

"No." With unbreakable steel in her eyes, she held my gaze without flinching. "It was hard to walk away from that money. It would have helped me out immensely. But I felt so degraded, so objectified. I don't expect to have the man of my dreams peel off my wedding dress before he makes love to me for the first time…but I didn't want my first time to be like that. I wanted it to mean something."

For a twenty-three-year-old, she had high expectations for something people tried to give away as soon as possible. Her self-respect for her virtue only made me want her more, because it had so much more value. "If it makes the rest of your life easier, that's all that matters. You aren't going to look back on that memory with regret. You're going to have more money in your pocket for the things that matter."

She shook her head slightly. "I don't understand. You're trying to convince me to change my mind, but another woman can replace me at the snap of a finger. She could meet you at your hotel in the next hour. So what are you doing?"

It was a great question. "I want you." It was the simplest, easiest answer.

Her eyes flicked down for a moment, like she couldn't handle the abrupt response. "Why?"

"I don't know. I just do." She was beautiful, but so were a lot of women. On the surface, there was nothing extraordinary about her. But underneath those looks was a special woman, a kind of person I'd never met before, someone who still thought the little things in life mattered. "And I think you'd be better off. You aren't going to find Mr. Perfect to sweep you off your feet and take your virginity in the most romantic way possible. At this age, any decent man wouldn't want to deal with that. And then the other dogs will just want to fuck you because you're a virgin."

"Like you?" she countered.

"Yes. But at least I know what I'm doing. And I'll fairly compensate you for it."

"Compensate me?" she asked with a laugh. "I feel like I'm selling eggs or cookies or something…"

It didn't seem like anything I said would change her mind. "You're attracted to me. You enjoy kissing me. Apparently, you enjoy having my dick in your mouth… So, why not?"

"Because you're an asshole." She stopped eating her chips and looked me dead in the eye. "You told me to shut up. You grabbed my head and fucked my mouth like I was a sex toy instead of a human being. It was so…robotic. It wasn't passionate or hot. It was just… I felt like a body. I never felt like a person."

That was exactly how I liked it, empty and meaningless. I liked taking a woman's virginity the way I fucked a whore. It was all about sex, all about getting off and feeling her tightness. I made them come because I was a natural at it, but it certainly wasn't romantic.

"No amount of money is worth being treated like that. I felt like a whore."

Because she was—an innocent whore.

"So, forget about me and find someone else who will be happy to do it."

She kissed me like she enjoyed it, so it made me wonder if I could have her if I treated her right. Maybe if I just asked her out on a date and bought her flowers, I could finally get what I wanted. But that seemed like too much work for a one-time fuck. "I'll make it $200,000."

She stared at me blankly, like she didn't understand a word I said.

"I'll double the payment if you reconsider." Regardless of how moral she was, that had to tempt her. That was a lot of money, even for a moderately wealthy person. She could remove a third of her debt. "That could wipe out all of your student loans. You would only be left with the medical expenses."

When she didn't turn me down right away, I knew she was considering it.

I waited patiently for her to give me an answer, to

tell me that was a fair price for her cherry. It was more than what I paid anyone else, but I knew it would be worth it.

That hatred entered her gaze. "You're an even bigger asshole than I thought. For a rich jerk like you, this is all a game. You buy whatever you want because you have so much money that it means nothing, but for people like me, I suffer every day because I didn't have a silver spoon in my mouth. Now you throw more money at me because you can, because you know I have no other option. You want my virginity because you get off on it, not caring if I have to sell my soul so you can have it. Instead of being a good person who helps someone in need, you use their struggle to your advantage. It's fucking despicable." She grabbed her purse and slipped out of the booth. "Fuck off, Slate Remington. Your money is no good here."

THE NEXT FEW days passed slowly.

Instead of thinking about Monroe's naked body on my bed, I thought about the last words she said to me.

When she put me in my place.

For a man who was incapable of feeling most emotions, I felt like shit. To me, this wasn't some sick game. This was a mutual benefit. She got what she wanted, and I got what I wanted. And it wasn't like my offer wasn't generous. Eventually, she would sleep with someone, be disappointed, and then regret not taking my offer.

Cherry Popper

Her words should have made me stop thinking about her instantly, but unfortunately, the exact opposite happened.

I wanted her so much, I was losing my mind.

I put the other women on hold because I needed to conquer Monroe before I could move forward. Right now, the only woman I wanted was out of my reach, and any other woman would just be a disappointment.

My first assistant, Jillian, came into my office. "Mr. Remington, here's everything you need for the meeting." She set a manila folder on my desk.

"Meeting?" I asked, drawing a blank because I'd spent so much time thinking about Monroe.

"Yes. Your brother is meeting you in ten minutes."

Shit, that was today? "Thank you, Jillian."

"Of course." She walked out.

I opened the folder and reviewed the numbers I would be presenting. My brother and I only spoke to each other on rare occasions, and only when it was necessary. Since we each owned half the company, we were forced to work together from time to time. He handled the resorts in the Middle and Far East, and I handled everything to the west. We had four quarterly meetings a year where we were forced to be face-to-face and a few other events that made us pretend not to despise each other. Today was a quarterly meeting, one I'd completely forgotten about.

I refused to dread it or be nervous. If anyone should feel threatened, it should be him. He was the one who'd fucked everything up—for a goddamn woman. The betrayal would always feel raw, like a wound that just couldn't heal. I tried not to live in the past or hold grudges, but when your flesh and blood stabbed you in the back, it was impossible to let go.

It wasn't even about her—it was about him.

I left my office and took the elevator down a few floors. When I stepped out of the elevator, I could see the glass walls of the conference room. It could hold fifty people comfortably, but for today, it would only hold the two of us.

I'd just happened to wear my best suit today and shave my beard, so I looked like a million bucks. I stepped through the door and found my brother standing at the head of the table, in a navy suit with a matching tie. There was no denying our relationship, not when we both had the same eyes, the same build, and features so similar, we looked like twins. His head was tilted down as he flipped through his notes.

That's when I noticed her.

Simone.

Tall, blond, and with vibrant blue eyes, she reminded me of a snake. She slithered in the dark and crept up on you in silence. Then she struck, sinking her fangs deep into your skin and injecting you with poison. She might be beautiful on the outside, but she was black as coal on the inside.

I hadn't expected to see her there because she was never present at our meetings, but I refused to look surprised. I walked to the table and sat down. "Ready?"

My brother finally glanced up from his folder to look at me, but he wore the same indifferent expression he'd consistently held all these years. Even though he brought her to my territory, he still didn't seem the least bit apologetic about it. "Yeah." He took a seat.

Simone sat in the seat across from me, decked out in expensive jewelry with perfectly styled hair. She wore a skintight black dress that showed her perfect figure. A diamond ring was on her left hand, a diamond so big it was impossible not to notice.

Jesus Christ.

"Coen, she has no business here." I looked at him and ignored her, pretending she wasn't there at all. "Last time I checked, we were the CEOs—and she was just your fuck buddy."

Coen lifted his gaze and looked at me, but he didn't rise to the insult I'd made about his woman. "Simone and I are getting married. That means she's a part of this company. She wants to be involved—which is why she's here."

I wanted to grab him by the neck and slam his face into the table. His lack of intelligence alarmed me at times. We all turned stupid when it came to good pussy, but his ignorance was terrifying. "Then tell her about your day when you get home."

"Half of the company will be hers—"

"Half of *half* the company will be hers," I corrected. "And you're an idiot for letting her have that much." The angrier I got, the more bitter I seemed, but my rage had nothing to do with my personal feelings toward her. If he brought in any woman off the street, I wouldn't be happy about it. But this woman, I knew exactly what she was after— our money. Coen didn't see it, but I certainly did.

"She has no experience or skills that give her the qualifications to sit at this table. This is *our* meeting." Having her around would only make things worse because she would whisper in his ear and subtly manipulate him, just the way she'd already manipulated both of us in the past.

Coen was wrapped around her finger too tight. "Let it go, Slate."

"Let what go?" I barked. "Even if I was fine with this, she's not your wife. You aren't married yet." I turned back to her. "So get the fuck out, or I'll throw you out."

Simone kept up her indifferent expression, like she didn't care about what I said at all.

If I had lesser morals, I would grab her by the neck and drag her out. "Coen, get rid of your whore."

"She's not a whore," he snapped.

"If she's slept with every man in the room, then yes, she's a fucking whore. And if you want me to stop talking about her like this, I suggest you get rid of her."

Coen and I weren't afraid to throw fists at each other's faces, but since we were at work and in a conference room made of glass, we behaved ourselves. He sighed before turning to his fiancée. "Wait for me in the lobby."

The heavy disappointment appeared in her eyes. "What did we—"

"I need to speak to Slate alone. Simone, go."

Clearly pissed that she wasn't getting her way like a brat, she grabbed her folder and stormed off, her heels clacking against the tile and announcing her rage. When the door shut behind her and her obnoxious heels turned silent, she was finally gone.

Coen turned to me. "It's been five years, Slate. You still aren't over it?"

"I never needed to get over it in the first place, asshole. She's a vindictive, manipulative, gold digger. How do you not see it? You don't think she pulled this same shit with me? When I didn't give her what she wanted, she moved on to you. How stupid are you?"

"It's not like that—"

"Yes, it is. Normally, I wouldn't care. If anything, you deserve everything that bitch is about to do to you. But this affects me—because half this company is mine. She's not qualified to play a CEO."

"Because she's a woman?" he asked incredulously.

"No. Because she's a bitch. I own half this company —and I want her to have nothing to do with it."

"There's not much I can do about that once we're married."

"She's signing a prenup. Easy solution."

"I can't ask her to sign that."

I raised an eyebrow. "Why the hell not?"

"It's offensive."

"No, it's necessary. The only reason you don't want to ask her is because you know she'll throw a fit. If she really loved you for you, she would sign the damn thing —and we both know it. I'm not letting that cunt walk in here and touch the company I've busted my ass for."

He drummed his fingers on the table as he looked at me.

"It's bad enough that you stabbed me in the back in

the first place. Now, this? What the fuck is wrong with you?" I grabbed my folder and shoved it into his chest. "Here are my numbers for the quarter. You can send yours via email—so I don't have to listen to this bullshit anymore."

I stormed out of the office and came face-to-face with Simone near the elevator. She stood perfectly upright with her folder tucked under her arm, trying to pretend she was more important than she really was.

I hit the button. "I know what you're doing, and it's not going to work."

"Really?" she asked. "What am I doing?"

"You're trying to sink your claws into our cash. You get half his portion and then start screwing some other guy. Coen is getting a prenup, so your genius idea won't work."

"Prenup, huh?" she asked. "Coen would never do that. He loves me—really loves me."

Because he was an idiot.

She stepped closer to me, her red lipstick contrasting against the fairness of the rest of her skin. "Does it still bother you? After all this time?" she whispered under her breath, her voice sultry.

My brother and I used to be much closer. We were more than just brothers—we were friends. But then he started fucking Simone behind my back while I was seeing her. When I found out about it, he started dating her publicly, making a scandal that buried us for years. At the time, I felt like a fool for letting Simone play me, but what hurt the most was my brother's betrayal. He traded in our relationship for a cheating whore. If we'd broken up and some time had passed before he'd asked if he could date her, I wouldn't have cared. But they'd both screwed me over. Simone wanted me for my money, but when she realized I would never marry her, she moved on to the next best thing—but my brother was too dense to see it. "Yes. It hurts knowing my brother is still this stupid—after all this time."

8

Monroe

I sat across from the finance guy at the bank, the company that held my student loans as well as my medical bills. Two hundred thousand dollars would have wiped out my student loans, but my pride was too big. I didn't want to submit to an asshole who thought he could have whatever he wanted.

The banker was an older man in a stuffy suit, flipping through my paperwork with a bored look on his face. "There's nothing that can be done. Since these are two private loans, they can't be consolidated into one. You might be able to find another company that might buy it out, but the debt ratio is so high that it's too risky."

I'd thought if I could refinance my loans, I could survive a little easier. Looked like that wouldn't happen. "Alright..."

He closed the folder then looked at me expectantly, like he wanted me to leave.

"Well…my student loans are only for ten years, right?" At least I wouldn't have to suffer like this forever.

"No. That's not correct."

My eyebrows furrowed. "But I'm on the ten-year plan."

"Yes…but you're making the minimum payments. So you're covering the interest but not the principle. At this rate…you'll be paying this off for an additional fifteen years."

"You've got to be fucking kidding me."

He stilled at my profanity. "I wish I were, miss."

"That's twenty-five years. That's a mortgage."

He nodded. "Student loans have exceeded credit card debt in this country. It's a crisis." He said it in a monotone voice, like he said this a million times a day to other people in my situation. "The only solution is to pay more money. If you doubled your payment every month, you could finish on time."

"That would mean I would have to pay thirty-five hundred dollars a month…" That was how much I made every month after taxes. "I literally can't afford that. It's not possible."

"Then I don't know what to say. It is what it is."

"Ugh…" I sat back in the chair and covered my face with my hand. Crying seemed so tempting, but I wouldn't do it out in public like this. I had more balls than that. "This is a fucking nightmare."

"I'm sorry," he said, like he didn't mean it at all. "And your private loan is nonnegotiable."

The loan for my mother's treatment had an insane interest rate since I already had so much debt from my student loans. I would be paying that until I died, and then it would be transferred to my children. That bill would hang over my head forever. Even if I could afford a down payment on a house, I could never actually buy one because no bank would give me a mortgage at this point.

How did I fuck up my life this much?

"I don't know what else to say. You could always get a second job."

And work sixteen hours a day, sleep, and then do it again the next day. "Thank you for your time." I grabbed the paperwork and walked out, feeling much worse than when I walked in the door.

Now Slate's offer was even more tempting. If I just put out, that would save me twenty-five years of student loan payments. Maybe I had no room to call the shots. Maybe I had no right to anything anymore. Maybe I needed to just stop believing in fairy tales and accept the cold, harsh reality of the world.

That life wasn't fair.

―――

I NEVER GOT Slate's phone number and I had no idea where he lived, so I had to go by his office again—even though his blond assistant would be pissed.

It was the second time I'd entered his office, and this time, the humiliation was even worse. I'd told him off and made a big speech about how he was an asshole, and now I was back because I was desperate.

He probably didn't even want to see me anymore.

He could just move on to someone else and forget about me.

He would probably lower the price now that he had all the power.

But if he was still interested, I could probably talk him back to two hundred. I really needed to get that loan cleared. Otherwise, I'd have to get a second job. My entire purpose in life would be just to work.

I stepped inside and saw the blond girl look at me, this time with fire in her eyes. She immediately rose to her feet, prepared to make my life a living hell.

I walked right past her.

"No, I don't think so." This time, she jumped over the counter, not caring about her dress riding up, and grabbed me by the arm. "This is not how this office works. You can't just march in here without an appointment—"

"Jillian." His deep voice immediately calmed her. In a gray suit and a black tie, he stood over both of us, acting as the thermostat in the room. He immediately lowered the temperature, making everyone cool down. "Miss Monroe is welcome to come and go as she pleases."

Jillian dropped my arm and became sweet as tea. "Of course, Mr. Remington. Thanks for letting me know." She walked away and returned to her desk.

I was relieved he'd saved me from her viciousness. "I'm sorry to drop by. I don't have your phone number…"

"I'll make sure to give it to you this time." He

stepped to the side and raised his arm to show me to the doors. "After you."

I tried not to roll my eyes as I stepped inside his office, annoyed by his gentlemanly façade in front of his employees. He was the most arrogant asshole I'd ever met, and the fact that he hid that from the public just annoyed me even more.

He shut the door behind me and sat behind his desk. "I have to say, I wasn't expecting to see you again." He relaxed in the chair, his elbows on the armrests and his fingers linked together. He wasn't as aggressive as he used to be, but his thick muscularity still made him intimidating. Those chocolate eyes always seemed sinister, and his jawline was so sharp, it could be used as a weapon. He'd shaved that morning, so all the angular lines were visible. He was the most beautiful man I'd ever seen, but he'd been swallowed by the shadows that existed in his eyes. He was no Prince Charming. He was the evil and sinister brother.

"Neither did I," I said honestly. "And I'm sorry to bother you at work."

"You aren't bothering me. I could use the distraction right now." He sighed quietly, his eyes taking on an air of annoyance.

"Why?"

"Just a bunch of bullshit. Nothing you'd be interested in."

Since I was only there for one reason, I didn't ask. "I went to the bank yesterday to consolidate my loans. They're out of control. I thought I could refinance them or something. But I found out that I'm going to be paying them off a lot longer because I can only afford the minimum payment…and it's just a nightmare."

He wore the same expression, not showing sympathy or irritation.

"Which brings me here…the last place I want to be." Women usually did the walk of shame after a long night of dirty deeds, but not before. Somehow, I was doing it backward. "So…here I am." I could barely look him in the eye because of the embarrassment. I'd made a big fuss about his money being worthless, and now I was asking for it again.

To my surprise, he didn't throw that back in my face. He didn't ask for an apology either. He just stared at me. "I still want to fuck you—if that's what you're asking."

He reminded me how harsh it would be with his choice of words. It wouldn't even be sex—but a fuck. He would pay for me then use me, use me like a disposable product. Once the packaging had ripped, it would never be the same. It was such a misogynistic view, this obsession with an untouched woman. It was a conquest, another accomplishment he could put on his resume. And I was going to give him what he wanted.

"You're sure you want to do this?" he asked. "Because I'm not interested in being teased anymore."

"Yes…but I have some stipulations."

He raised an eyebrow.

"I don't want to be bossed around. I don't want to be told to shut up. I don't want—"

"Let's not forget I'm paying a fortune to enjoy you. So I can do and say whatever the fuck I want." He turned cold, cold like he'd been the first time we met. "This is my fantasy, my fetish. If I want you to shut up, you'll shut up. If I want you on your knees, you'll get on the floor. This is a transaction, a service you're providing me. And I want the experience that I'm paying for. Understand?"

I kept my mouth shut, my anger rising to the surface. I didn't appreciate being spoken to like that, but I shouldn't have expected anything less. Sometimes Slate was kind and quiet, and in those moments, I forgot how huge of an asshole he could be. There were two different versions of him, one that kissed me and talked to me over sandwiches. Then there was this version… the mean and cold dictator.

"You get no stipulations, sweetheart. You take the money and let me do whatever I want. That's how this works."

The self-loathing returned, and I was tempted to walk out of there again. I didn't want my first time to be with a controlling asshole who treated something so intimate like sex with a prostitute, but now that my loans were an even bigger problem, I had no choice. I had to make this go away. Otherwise, I had absolutely no future.

He kept staring at me as he waited for my cooperation. He was absolutely still, stationary like a statue. His eyes didn't blink or shift, and that level of stillness was scary. He was like a predator that hid in plain sight. He was so quiet, you didn't realize he was there until it was too late.

"I understand…"

"Good. Then check in to the hotel like last time. I want you naked on the bed when I walk in."

9

Slate

I was hard in my jeans before I made it to the door.

I'd been waiting for this moment for nearly two weeks. I hadn't been with another woman in the meantime because I'd been so focused on getting in between Monroe's legs. Her resistance aroused me, but her surrender turned me on even more. I admired her for trying to do the right thing, but I loved it when her attempts failed. The power surged through my veins, and that only made my dick harder.

I'd finally conquered her.

I slid the card into the lock then stepped inside. The room was exactly as I liked it, and I spotted her dress and shoes near the dining table. Her panties were there too. I stood over them and stared, my cock pressing against the zipper in my pants. I opened my wallet and pulled out the check written in her name. I set it on top of her panties, knowing she would understand the significance when we were finished.

Then I stripped down, knowing she was naked on the bed and waiting for me. My cock was so eager to be inside her that it twitched in my boxers before I could get them off. I got down to my skin then made myself a drink—to celebrate.

I'd never wanted to fuck a virgin more.

I licked the scotch off my lips then stepped into the open bedroom.

As I'd asked, she leaned against the headboard with her knees pulled toward her body, obscuring her goods. Her arm was draped across her chest, hiding her tits from view. Her hair was curled, and she had dark makeup around her eyes, making them look smoky and sexy. Her eyes were filled with the same trepidation she showed last time, like she hated herself for doing this just for the money.

What she didn't understand was how much this would change her life—for the better. That money would make most of her problems go away. And the sex would be the best she would ever have. If only she trusted me.

I moved to the edge of the bed and grabbed her slender ankle. My thumb caressed the little bone, and I gently tugged on her extremity. She resisted me at first until she relaxed. I straightened her leg then grabbed the other. I gave a gentle tug, pulling her down the bed and closer to me.

My eyes roamed over her body, seeing her perfect waistline, her perfect tits, and that freshly shaved landing

Cherry Popper

strip. I moved farther onto the bed then gathered her legs in my arms. I pulled them apart, revealing her gorgeous slit. She wasn't oozing from her entrance like most woman would be, but once I had her warmed up, she would be ready for me.

Without asking for permission, I moved my face between her legs and kissed her.

Her belly rose with the breath she inhaled, and she let out a little scream of surprise. Her hands were on the bed on either side of her, and she automatically gripped the sheets when she felt my warm mouth against her nub.

I didn't spend a lot of time kissing a woman's cunt, but I'd been fantasizing about this for weeks. I sucked her little nub into my mouth and pulled gently, making her back arch instantly and her breathing quicken. My tongue circled the area before I continued kissing her, continued devouring her.

She finally relaxed once it started to feel good, and all the tightness in her back faded away. She breathed deep and hard and clawed at the sheets on either side of her. Soon, the moans began, sexy little sounds that filled the bedroom.

I kissed her hard and felt my dick swell like a balloon. I liked the way she tasted, the way she responded to me as if a man had never kissed her like this before. My tongue dived into her slit, and I felt her moisture start to flood her channel.

Maybe I wouldn't need lube after all.

Her moans grew regular, and she started to gently

rock her hips back into me, like she wanted more of my mouth.

I sucked her nub firmly, making her hips buck hard, and then I pulled away. I wanted to bring her to the verge of an orgasm so when I put my fat dick inside her, she would be able to come around me despite the pain.

I held myself on top of her with one arm then inserted a finger inside her. She was definitely wet, but I noticed something else. "Fuck, you're so tight." I saw my desire mirrored in her eyes, and even if I hadn't, I could certainly feel it on my finger. I leaned down and kissed her on the mouth as I continued to finger her, to get her cunt to relax enough so I could slip my big dick inside her next.

Her lips were unresponsive at first, probably because of the taste of my mouth. Maybe she'd never tasted herself before and it took a moment to ignore. Her mouth started to move with mine, and she panted as I fingered her, prepared her for the real thing. Her hands gripped my shoulders as she braced herself for what would happen next.

I was much more generous this time around because I didn't want her to ditch me again. So I showed her how good sex could really be—even without intercourse. I kissed her and fingered her for a while as I got her as hot as possible. More arousal flooded her entrance, and she started to rock back into my palm.

I was so fucking hard.

We hadn't even gotten to the fun part yet.

I pulled my finger out of her slit and ended the kiss. Now I couldn't wait to push through her tightness and

Cherry Popper

pop that cherry. I couldn't wait to feel that incredibly tight pussy, to watch her work to take me. I hoped she would cry, because that was the perfect thing to come to. I grabbed my dick and pressed my head against her small entrance. Her lower lips were uncooperative, so I would have to sink slowly until I could get her to stretch for me. She was smaller than usual, so it would take some time.

But I was a patient man.

I slowly pushed inside her, waiting several seconds before I could even get my head past her lips.

She gripped my arms and breathed hard as she allowed me to enter her. Her eyes were locked to mine and full of distress. She'd been aroused just seconds ago, but now her body was tightening everywhere.

"Stay with me, sweetheart." Once I was fully inside her, there was no going back. I would hold her down until I finished if I had to.

"I can't...this doesn't feel right."

"I'll make you come. I promise."

"No..." She pressed her hands against my chest. "Get off."

I stayed put, wanting to disobey her and do it anyway. No one would hear her screams, and she couldn't fight me off.

But I never wanted to be that guy. It was one thing to pay for pussy—another to take it without consent. "Fuck." I moved off her, my dick so hard it actually ached. I lay on my back and dragged my hands down my face, trying to bottle my frustration as best as I could.

She left the room and grabbed her clothes from the dining table.

I lay there, blowing smoke out of my nostrils while my hard cock continued to throb against my stomach. He was so hard, and the only way he would stop being hard was if he had an orgasm. It'd been two weeks since the last one.

Instead of storming out right away, she stood in the doorway and stared at me. "I'm sorry."

I stared at the ceiling and ignored her. I was too pissed off to talk. She'd teased me again, and an apology wouldn't make up for it. It drove me crazy every time I imagined finally fucking her, and she took that dream away over and over. I'd even doubled my offer for the opportunity, but she still wouldn't give it up. "Leave." I didn't raise my voice or project an angry tone. I just wanted her out of my sight—so I could beat off in peace.

But she continued to linger, unsure how to absolve her guilt.

I refused to make her feel better by telling her it was okay. It wasn't okay at all.

She set her purse down on the dining table then removed her dress again.

Now I turned still, even my breathing stopped. Maybe she'd changed her mind. Maybe this would happen after all.

Her knees hit the mattress, and she moved on top of me, beautifully naked and smooth. She arched her back in the sexiest way, bending like a cat, and she stuck her ass in the air as she brought her face to my dick. She wrapped her hand around the base then pointed my shaft at her mouth. Then she deep-throated me.

I closed my eyes when I felt her wetness and her warmth. It wasn't a pussy, but it was still damn good. Her tongue was flat, and her mouth was wide open with perfect form. I'd had my dick sucked a lot in life, and I knew a good blow job from a bad blow job in the first ten seconds.

This was a good one.

Her hair was all over the place as she bent her neck to take me over and over again. She pushed me deep before she pulled me out again, a line of saliva stretching from the head of my cock to the corner of her mouth. She swiped it away with her tongue then kept going, using her hand to jerk me off at the same time.

I propped myself on one arm so I could watch her suck me off, watch her get me soaking wet. My hand moved into her hair to keep it out of her face, and I guided her, showing her the exact pace I liked. I hoped she was getting me wet to fuck her, but I suspected I was just getting an apologetic blow job tonight.

I'd take it.

She massaged my balls as she continued to move up and down, pushing my long length deep into the back of her throat. She gave it her all, stopping herself from gagging more than once. Sometimes she heaved with her breaths when she took a break, but then she went right back to fucking me with her throat.

She gave good head.

My hand fisted her hair, and I breathed through the

goodness that started in my balls. "I'm gonna come, baby. And you're going to take all of me, as much as you can, and hold it as I finish."

When she kept going, I assumed that was her compliance.

I guided her mouth down my length with my final pumps, letting her breathe before I finished. Just as I released, I pulled her down far, making her take as much of me as possible. I didn't even allow her to breathe as I exploded inside her mouth, pretending it was her virgin pussy. I moaned with satisfaction as the intensity burned through my veins and left me feeling weak and strong at the same time. I couldn't see my come, but I could feel how much it was, how much was being dumped into her throat. When I finished, I finally let her go.

She pulled back and took a deep breath, filling her lungs with air and swallowing all the come I'd just released inside her.

I was still livid she'd turned me down, but at least she did something to make up for it.

She moved to her back beside me and wiped her mouth with the back of her hand. Instead of leaving right away, she lay beside me, beautiful and naked.

I stayed quiet as I enjoyed the aftershocks of pleasure. I'd had a lot of beautiful women give me great head, but nothing quite like that. Maybe it was because she was inexperienced that I was so impressed, but either way, I enjoyed it more than any other blowjob I'd ever received. "What was that for?" Did she suck my dick out of pity? Was she turned on but just didn't want to have sex?

"Is your dick that hard all the time?"

"Just around you."

"I couldn't stop staring at it. He seemed so disappointed."

"He *is* disappointed." I stared at the ceiling as my breathing slowly returned to normal.

"I thought I did a good job…"

"That's not why he's disappointed, Monroe. You've come to me twice now and offered yourself. Then you take it away. It's the worst tease in the world. Make up your fucking mind. Are we doing this or not?"

"I…I don't know."

Not the answer I was looking for. "I'm not going to offer you more money, if that's what your game is." Maybe this was all a big ploy to get me to pay her as much as possible. I'd been tricked before.

"It's not," she said quietly. "Every time I think I'm brave enough to do it…I get scared."

"There's nothing to be scared of."

"Yes, there is. I'm scared of regret."

"Most women regret their first time, no matter what. Just how most women regret every relationship they've ever been in, no matter what. You're overthinking it."

"I just think I deserve better…"

She did deserve better.

"Coming to this hotel room…just makes it seem trashy. This is the bed where you popped all their cherries. There's a picture of a cherry on the wall, for Christ's sake. It just feels wrong. It feels…gross."

"You want to come to my place instead? Would that make it better?"

"I guess it would feel more personal…"

"Then I'm willing to do that."

"But it still doesn't feel right. I don't even know you."

"I'm not that interesting," I said, wanting to skip the conversation and go right for the kill.

"I still don't know you. It would be easier if I at least knew you, respected you, even liked you…"

I should just give up on this girl and move on, but I was still looking for any way to make this happen. "What are you suggesting? That I date you? The whole reason I pay for pussy is so I don't have to do that."

"Not date me," she said. "Maybe just be my friend…"

I didn't have any friends.

"Could we get to know each other first? Could we fool around first? Could we build up to the moment?"

So I would pay her double, and I would have to wine and dine her first. That didn't sound like an arrangement I wanted. That sounded like the exact thing I wanted to avoid. But it seemed like if I wanted to get between her legs, that was the only way to make it happen. "Alright."

She turned to me, surprise in her beautiful eyes. "Really?"

"Yeah." I would bend over backward to fuck this girl—and I hoped she'd be worth it.

"You can still do what you were doing before in the meantime…it's not like I'm asking you to give that up while you wait."

"I assumed." Not that I would continue anyway.

When I fucked a woman, I only thought of her until the moment was over. Then I forgot about her and moved on to the next. But with Monroe, she was the only woman on my mind at the moment, the only conquest I wanted to make.

"We can go back to your original offer. Now that we're doing this, it doesn't seem fair—"

"I stand by my offer. So how does this work? We spend time together, and then you tell me when you're ready?"

"Yeah…I guess."

"I'm not trying to be an ass, but this better not take longer than a month."

"I guess we'll see…"

10

Monroe

I wasn't playing games.

When I met him at the hotel, I really thought I would go through with it.

But it still didn't feel right. I felt trapped, like I was doing it for the wrong reasons. It felt like a regret even though I hadn't even gone through with it yet. The man paying me for my virginity was practically a stranger. I knew hardly anything about him besides his first and last name.

That didn't feel right either.

When I told my boyfriend or lover about my first time, I wanted to say positive things about the guy. At least I could say he was my friend and someone I respected and admired. Maybe we weren't in love, but we trusted each other. That was much better than screwing a stranger for money.

It would help me sleep at night.

I was sitting at my desk working on an ad for an

editorial when my assistant knocked on my office door. "Uh, Monroe. There's a man here to see you…and I'm pretty sure it's Slate Remington. I mean, it looks just like him. He's wearing a suit and everything." Wide-eyed and with stars in her gaze, she seemed smitten by what she saw. "Do you know him?"

"Actually, I do know him. But I can't imagine why he would stop by my office like this."

"Wants to know if you're free for lunch."

"Really?" After I'd turned him down, I figured he wouldn't want to see me for a week. It'd only been a few days since that night at the hotel, but maybe he wanted to make progress sooner rather than later—so he could fuck me. I didn't understand his obsession with getting me into bed. The only person who should be obsessed with it is me—because he was the gorgeous one. If I weren't a virgin, I would probably pay him to sleep with me.

"Yeah. He's standing by my desk."

"Tell him I'll be right there." I finished what I was working on and then put my computer to sleep before I grabbed my coat and walked to my assistant's desk outside in the main lobby. Since I worked in fashion, we were more laid-back around the office, wearing cute outfits rather than pantsuits and jackets. Today I wore a red dress with a jean jacket and flats. My hair was curled and pulled back into a ponytail. When I rounded the corner and saw him, perfectly filling out his suit with a face so handsome he should be a model for the company, I suddenly felt ugly in what I was wearing.

I walked up to him, feeling the muscles tighten in my

chest when I remembered how his come tasted in my mouth. I'd only caught a little bit of it because most of it went straight into my throat, but it was potent enough to leave a lingering effect. When I stopped in front of him, I felt my stomach drop into the bottom part of my body, a weight of nervousness hitting me. I forced a smile. "Where did you have in mind?"

"Ladies' choice." He walked with me out of the office, keeping space between us like we were colleagues. We took the elevator down to the bottom floor and then walked out onto the sidewalk, joining the thousands of other people on the hunt for lunch.

"Well, I could eat anything. I'm not picky. You're the one who won't eat carbs, so you tell me."

He chuckled slightly. "There's this little café I like. It's right over here. They've got great salads."

I stuck out my tongue. "I'm not eating a salad for lunch." I was starving most of the time, so I wanted real food.

"They have sandwiches and pasta too."

"Oh…then I'm in."

We walked inside, ordered our food, and then took a seat. Slate paid for me without giving me the opportunity to even grab my wallet.

The first few times he'd paid, it didn't seem like a big deal. But if we were going to be spending more time together, it didn't seem right to let him pay all the time. Even if I overdrafted my account, it was better than mooching off of him. "I get the next one, alright?"

"No." He stabbed his fork into his kale salad with chicken and walnuts.

"No?" I challenged. "I'm not one of your employees. I'm a person."

"You see the way I talk to my employees—and that's not how. And the answer is still no."

"If we're going to keep spending time together, I don't think it's fair that you—"

He leaned forward as he looked me in the eye. "No means no. It's nothing against you. It just makes me very uncomfortable when people pay for my things."

"Why?"

"Does it matter why?" He took a bite of his salad.

"I'm getting to know you, so yes. It does matter."

"Alright." He finished chewing before he gave his answer. "I'm a very wealthy man who's never had to live on a budget. Seeing someone less fortunate than I am buy my food…doesn't sit right with me. I'm not being a gentleman. I just…don't like it."

"So if I were richer than you, you wouldn't mind?"

He shrugged. "I've never met someone richer than me."

Both of my eyebrows shot up. "How rich are you?"

"I just mean, I haven't gone out to eat with someone wealthier who then offered to buy my food." He kept eating, enjoying his low-carb, low-fat salad.

I got a foot-long pastrami sandwich. I was used to being broke all the time, so anytime I ate, I ate as much as possible. It was a bad habit. "So if I ever become richer than you, you'd let me buy your food?"

He grinned at the thought. "Maybe not…"

"So you are a gentleman."

"No. I just like you." His phone vibrated in his pocket, so he checked the screen before he put it back.

I smiled at the comment. "You like me?"

"I don't think I would go through all this trouble to fuck you if I didn't."

"What do you like about me?" I set my sandwich down and watched him, seeing the way his brown eyes darkened when he considered his answer. Now that the pressure of putting out was off the table, I felt like I could be myself, see him as a person rather than a predator.

"Is this grade school?"

"I'm just curious."

"If I answer your question, you have to answer the same."

"Why I like myself?" I asked blankly.

"Why you like me. We've got a deal?"

"Sure."

"Alright." He took a few more bites of his salad before he spoke. "You're beautiful, for one. That's the first thought that popped into my head when you walked into my office, uninvited."

"You thought I was pretty? You looked like you wanted to murder me."

He pointed to his face. "That's just how I look. I look pissed all the time."

"Trust me, you do not. You're smiling right now."

"Well, that's because you're giving me a reason to. Now I have more reasons. Do you want to hear them?"

"Yes."

"Alright," he said. "I like that you're selfless. You did

the best thing for your mom regardless of the consequences. That's pretty damn noble."

My smile disappeared when I thought of my mother, who'd been gone for over a year now.

He continued. "You're a hard worker. You worked your ass off to survive in Manhattan. Regardless of your financial situation, you're an executive with an assistant at a big company. That's not easy to pull off."

I never thought about it that way.

"And the last reason is because you didn't give it up to guys who didn't deserve it. If you put out too soon, you would have regretted it. But you waited long enough to find out if the guys were worthy—which they weren't. Also noble."

"You said waiting was pointless."

"I still believe that. But unlike everyone else in the world, you think your virginity actually means something. So you want to give it to the right person. That innocence is naïve, but also endearing. And that makes me want to take it from you…because it's so valuable. I understand that makes me an asshole, but that's what I'm into. I like being a woman's first memory of sex. I like knowing she'll never forget me."

It did make him a bit of an asshole, but at least he was honest about it.

"Why do you like me?" he asked. "I suspect this list will be shorter than mine."

"Well, the most obvious reason…you're gorgeous." I could barely look him in the eye as I said it, especially when he grinned like he got his favorite toy on Christmas morning. "You've got those masculine features in your face…that jawline…and then everything under your clothes is nice too. And that dick…not sure how I'm gonna take that."

His smile dropped within the snap of a finger, and the same dark expression he'd shown in the office returned. Now he turned intense, his eyes focused on me with such concentration that he didn't even blink. "You will take it, sweetheart."

I felt the steam come out of my ears, and the heat grow under the collar of my jacket. He could be playful one moment and then turn into the intense man who longed to fuck me in the next. "Anyway…I liked how sincere you seemed when I told you what happened to my parents. You have a heart under all that hostility. I know it's there even if you try to hide it. I think you're a good kisser. And I like that you're honest, even if it doesn't paint you in the best light. Honesty is so rare these days that it practically doesn't exist. But with you…I never have to wonder how you feel about something. No matter how terrible your opinion is, you'll say it out loud." I grabbed my sandwich again. "That's about it…"

"I was hoping you would like me because I buy you food."

I chuckled. "It doesn't hurt…but that's not why I like you."

We ate in comfortable silence, stealing glances at each other across the table. His mind seemed to be racing behind his eyes, because he eventually said, "Has a man ever gone down on you before?"

I felt the heat creep up my neck. "Why do you ask?"

"You seemed to enjoy it."

"Is there a woman in the world who doesn't enjoy that?"

"Answer the question."

I was embarrassed to comply. "No…"

"That was your first time?"

"Yes."

Most of his salad had been eaten, so he set his fork on his tray and put his entire focus on me. "I'm surprised. You have a nice pussy."

"Thanks…you have a nice dick."

"I think they'll go well together."

I wasn't so sure about that part. He was so thick and long that it probably would hurt the entire time. We would have to do it at least a dozen times before I could actually enjoy it, but since he only screwed virgins, that didn't seem possible. "So, what can you tell me about your family?"

"My father died about ten years ago. Heart attack."

"Oh…I'm sorry."

He didn't seem too sad about it. "My mom is still around. She's a socialite in the city."

"Socialite?" I asked, having no idea what that meant.

"She's a rich person who hangs with the popular crowd, basically."

"Is she rich because you're rich? Or was she rich before?"

"I come from a wealthy family," he admitted. "My father started the company I own now. It was much smaller at the time, but my brother and I turned it into the behemoth it is today. Now we have luxury hotels all over the world with top-of-the-line service. My father was successful but small-minded. I transformed it into something better."

"I heard that you and your brother have bad blood."

"Don't believe everything you read," he said. "But yes, that's true."

"That's too bad."

He shrugged and didn't elaborate. "We keep it professional."

"But you don't have a relationship outside of work?"

"Not at all."

"What about the holidays?"

"We get together for my mom. But that's it. Once she's gone, we'll stop the charade."

I couldn't imagine hating a family member. "What happened?"

He shook his head like he wasn't going to answer. "I don't want to talk about it."

"We're getting to know one another. You think I'm going to judge you?"

"No. I just don't want to talk about it." He held my gaze with ferocity, like he dared me to ask him again.

I didn't. "So you took over the family business the second you were an adult?"

"No. I took a few years off and traveled across Europe."

"Ooh…that sounds fascinating."

"Yes, I had a good time. I returned to the States a couple years later, took over the company with Coen, and then my father dropped dead from a heart attack.

Now it's been almost a decade and so much has changed."

"Yeah…I can only imagine. How's your mother?"

"She's good. Had a few boyfriends but I chased them off."

"Why would you chase them off?" I asked with a laugh.

"They weren't good enough for her. They only wanted her for her money. I really dig into the guys that show interest in my mom to make sure they're being genuine."

"That's sweet…"

"I hope she meets a good guy eventually. I want her to have a companion. My father died young, but she's got a long way to go."

"When the time is right, I'm sure it'll happen."

"Maybe," he said noncommittally. "So, I'm guessing you want the house, kids, and the white picket fence."

"You say it like it's a bad thing."

"No. It was just a question."

"But your tone was pretty stern there."

He shrugged. "You know I'm not a fan of monogamy."

"Well, yes. I do want all those things—minus the picket fence. Those are a bit out of style."

He chuckled. "True."

"I was thinking of a townhouse in the city. Something big enough for the kids to run around in, something close to the good schools, and something reasonably close to work. But with my debt following me everywhere I go, that may never happen."

"A real man isn't going to care about that."

"I would," I argued. "If a guy told me he was $600,000 in debt, I'd run."

"But you're a woman, so it's different."

"How so?"

"The man is supposed to take care of the woman, not the other way around. If he was stupid enough to get stuck in that situation, then he doesn't have the qualifications to be a good partner anyway."

Both of my eyebrows arched as I was deeply offended by what he said.

It took him a second to understand my reaction. "That's not what I meant. Don't take it out of context."

"Why else would he be $600,000 in debt?"

"Gambling. Most men get into debt from gambling, not student loans. It's a sad statistic, but true nevertheless. I don't think getting an education should ever be a mistake. Something needs to be done about the problem because we have a lot of young people who want to better themselves, but now it's impossible to do that. It's a scary thought, because we need working professionals in our lives."

"True."

"I don't think you're stupid," he repeated. "That came out wrong."

I knew he wouldn't lie to me, so I let it be. "Since you bought me lunch, I'll let you off the hook."

He smiled. "That's a fair trade."

I pulled out my phone and looked at the time. "I should get back to work. I've got a lot of stuff to do today."

"Alright." He left the booth and carried the trays to the garbage can. Then he walked with me outside. "Would you like to come to my place for dinner tonight? I'm making chicken Marsala."

"A home-cooked meal?" I asked, immediately enticed.

"Is that a yes?"

I told him I didn't want my first time to be in that hotel room where all the other women lost their V-cards. We decided to do it at his place instead, and knowing we would be alone together over dinner made me feel the pressure.

He must have detected my unease. "Until you explicitly tell me you're ready, I won't try to make it happen."

That was a relief. I'd thought I would have to keep my guard up the entire time. Having lunch with him was so nice because there were no expectations. We couldn't sneak off into the bathroom and hook up. "Then I'd love to."

"Great. And just to clarify, even though we won't be having sex tonight, that doesn't mean I won't be all over you. Because I will be *all* over you."

11

Slate

It was the first time I'd had a woman at my apartment.

This penthouse was my safe haven, the place I retreated to avoid people and bullshit.

But I wanted to spend time with her, and I didn't always want to do that in public. She didn't want to go to the hotel, and if she was that uncomfortable, I wasn't going to force it.

By the time I had dinner ready, she'd ridden the elevator to my floor and stepped inside the large living room that could easily fit twenty guests comfortably. She looked around like she couldn't believe what she was seeing and then walked up to me. "Your living room is bigger than my entire apartment."

I didn't find her financial situation funny, so I didn't respond. "I hope you're hungry." Sometimes when I first greeted her, I was tempted to kiss her like a lover, but I never did because it seemed inappropriate. She wasn't my girlfriend, so I shouldn't treat her like she was. When we started fooling around, my mouth would be all over her. But when I greeted her at the door, it felt misleading to kiss her, especially when she was just a friend.

"Always."

I put the plates on the table, along with a bottle of red wine. I poured the glasses then sat across from her. The dining table was in the corner of the space, so it had glass walls on either side, revealing a breathtaking view of the city by night. All you could see were endless white lights from the buildings and red taillights from the traffic down on the roads.

She cut into her chicken and took a bite. "Wow, this is good."

"Why do you seem so surprised?"

"I figured you had a maid cook for you."

"No. I have a maid take care of the house when I'm at work. But I prepare my own meals."

"That's interesting."

"Why?"

She shrugged. "You're so busy that the last thing you probably want to do is cook."

"I'd rather cook than have someone in my apartment while I'm here. I'm not a people person."

"Not a people person?" She wore jeans and a blouse, her first outfit that wasn't a dress or skirt. Her hair was curled around her shoulders, and she looked energetic, like she hadn't been at work all day. "What does that mean?"

"Exactly as it sounds. I don't like people."

"Like, all people?" she asked, still eating. "You work in hospitality, so how is that possible?"

"I know how people want to be treated. But that doesn't mean I want to be the one to treat them that way."

Instead of calling me bitter and sad, she just accepted it. "Any particular reason why?"

"I think people are terrible—as a species."

"Are you including yourself in this?"

"Definitely." I was one of the biggest assholes I'd ever met.

"I think people can be evil, but I think people can be good too. You shouldn't focus on only the evil and forget about the good entirely."

I lived at the top of the food chain, so I knew how the real world worked. I knew that corporations purposely misled people for financial gain, that all people cared about was making money, even at the expense of human life. I saw how the wealthy treated the middle class like they were dogs. I saw the way my own brother slept with my girlfriend behind my back and never had the balls to tell me about it. He was my own flesh and blood, my family, but pussy was more important than loyalty. "The whole reason you're stuck in this loan nightmare is because rich people just want to make money off you. They want young people to make these mistakes, so they can profit off you the second you graduate college. Then you can't afford to buy property, so you rent somewhere, but then the rent keeps on increasing because they know you'll sacrifice more and more just to have a place to live. The world is full of terrible people who will trample anyone in their way on the path to the top."

The fork and knife were in her hands, but she stopped eating so she could stare at me. She slowly lowered her utensils, giving me a focused expression. "That's a bleak outlook."

"It's the truth. Sadly. The American dream died almost a hundred years ago."

"What about your family? Your dad must have had nothing when he started."

"No. My grandfather was the president of a banking company. He loaned my father the money to start his own hotel chain. They say the rich get richer…which is entirely true."

"If you're in this elite club, why do you sound so bitter about it?"

Everything traced back to my brother, the real source of my anger. Simone meant something to me when we were together. She stayed at my place the entire time, and it was the only relationship I'd ever had. When she screwed me over, I immediately forgot about her. I didn't let her hurt me more than she already had. But seeing my brother still stand by her after all these years…just reminded me how he'd betrayed me in the first place. Maybe I would never get over it. "I have my reasons."

"Care to share?" She went back to eating.

"Not really. I don't want to spoil the evening."

"Because you haven't already?" she asked with a laugh. "I'm the one stuck in the situation, but I'm not nearly as bitter about it as you are. You can let the

Cherry Popper

weight of your grief pull you down, or you can keep going and hope things get better."

For most people, it never got better. "How was your day?"

"Trying to change the subject?"

"Unless you want me to keep ruining the evening."

"Even when you're saying depressing things, you look sexy while you talk, so it's not that bad." She wore a playful smile as she looked down at her plate and cut into her asparagus.

Even when I was in my worst mood, she managed to pick me up. "So, how was your day?"

"Good. The office was crazy busy. We're getting ready for the winter selection."

"Isn't fall next?"

"Yes, but we finished fall in spring."

"So you do opposite seasons?" I asked.

"Exactly. Always ahead of the game. How was your day?"

I had to deal with that leech Simone. My brother didn't recognize she was a gold digger because he was balls deep in her pussy. She probably didn't love my brother at all. She tried to pressure me into marriage, and when I wasn't stupid enough to fall for her act, she went after my gullible brother instead.

As if a woman like that would really love him.

The second she owned a part of our company, she would leave him.

Coen was a pussy and wouldn't be able to face her in the office.

So I would be stuck with her, dealing with a tramp while running the company.

If he didn't sign that prenup, I would beat him until he was at the pearly gates.

I finally answered her. "Busy."

"How do you manage so many hotels all over the world?"

"With managers," I said. "I do administrative stuff. My brother controls the east side of the world, and I control the west. We compare numbers every quarter. We basically just count the money and make sure there are no issues going on."

"Do you visit your hotels often?"

"Sometimes. I don't travel as much as I should."

"Then maybe you need to start." She ate everything on her plate, not even leaving the greens behind.

If she really ate like this at every meal, she wouldn't be so thin. That made me wonder if she could even afford to eat. Maybe the only meals she was eating were the ones she had with me.

The thought made me sick.

When we finished dinner, I left the dishes in the sink. They'd be washed the next day when the maid came, so I didn't bother. But I brought the bottle and glasses to the table in the living room so we could keep drinking.

"I didn't realize you liked wine." She sat beside me and crossed her legs. "It seems like you're always drinking liquor."

"I have wine with dinner sometimes." I took a long sip to cleanse my palate before I set the glass on the table. Now that the lights were low and her belly was full, all I could think about was my deep attraction to her, the way I longed to drag my bottom lip up her neck before I gave her a deep kiss. I wanted to press my face between those plump tits and lick the valley created by them. I wanted to smell her perfume, smell her cunt.

She took a drink as she kept her eyes on me, becoming noticeably quiet as she waited for me to make good on my threat.

"Put the glass down." I wished she'd worn a dress so I could get to her pussy faster. Actually, I wished she'd arrived in nothing but a trench coat so I could enjoy her the second she walked into the room.

She set it on the table then turned back to me.

"Now strip." I preferred to take this into the bedroom, but if we were on a bed, she might think I was trying to fuck her. The couch would work perfectly well for what I had in mind.

She stilled like she might not obey. Then she slowly pulled her blouse over her head, unclasped her bra, and then stood up to unfasten her jeans.

I wouldn't be coming in her pussy tonight, but I'd be coming somewhere—maybe on her tits.

She pushed her jeans to her ankles then stepped out of them. Then she worked the sexy white thong, pulling it over her hips and down her long legs. She stepped out of it and left her clothes in a pile on the floor. Beautiful from head to toe, she had the most amazing proportions. She had long legs, big tits, and a petite frame. Instead of being a marketing executive, she should be one of the models for her company.

"I can't wait to pop your cherry, sweetheart." I

undid the front of my jeans because now they were too snug with my thick cock. He needed more room to come alive, more room to throb with desire.

She eyed my cock with the same longing look I gave her.

I lifted my hips and pushed my jeans and boxers down to my thighs. Then I pulled my shirt over my head, revealing my muscled chest for her to enjoy. "Come here. I want to show you something." I patted my thigh.

She came toward me, her leg touching my knee.

I grabbed her hand and yanked her on top of me, forcing her knees to separate and hug my hips. I pulled her close to me, positioning her pussy to sit right on top of my shaft.

Her hands pressed against my chest as she breathed hard while she waited for whatever I had planned next.

"I want to show you how good it's going to feel." I pulled her face to mine and kissed her as my hips started to move. I gripped her hips and guided her body in the right way, making her clit grind against my rock-hard dick. Our movements were slow because she didn't understand what we were doing at first, but once she felt the stimulation in the right spot, she inhaled a deep breath and dug her nails into my chest. I watched her eyes light up with pleasure, watched her feel something she'd never felt before.

She started to move with me, began to guide her body down my shaft then up again. Her breathing quickened, and she moved her lips with mine, slowly

Cherry Popper

kissing me as she felt the wonderful pleasure down below.

Her juice smeared my length, made it wet, slippery, and sticky.

Man, I couldn't wait to fuck her.

Knowing she was so wet in that moment aroused me beyond belief.

She moved a little quicker, keeping up our embrace as her clit throbbed against my big dick. Her nails expressed her enthusiasm when her kiss didn't, and soon she was breathing hard against my mouth, like a climax was just over the horizon.

"There you go, sweetheart." I pushed against her and ground hard, giving her an epic push to set off an orgasm she would never forget. We'd just scratched the surface of pleasure, and it would be so much better once I was inside her. I wanted to give her something to look forward to, something to chase away her doubt. Because she and I would be incredible together.

She locked her arms around my neck and bucked her hips uncontrollably, her body spasming as she enjoyed the climax that made her toes curl against my thighs. A scream left her lips and washed across my face, her pleasure as audible as a ringing bell. Her nails nearly drew blood in her excitement, and her hips didn't stop bucking until the hurricane had passed.

Now she was just a crumpled mess in front of me, satisfied and exhausted. My dick was still hard underneath her, warm and throbbing. Her arms dropped from around my neck and she explored my chest, feeling the hard muscle underneath. A slight redness from embarrassment came into her cheeks, as if she couldn't believe what had just happened. She lowered her gaze, the sweat gleaming on her beautiful collarbone and chest. Her fingertips continued to caress me as she sat there and recovered from the aftershocks.

The last time I dry-humped was in high school, and I hadn't realized how sexy it could be—with the right person. Everything was new for Monroe, including the moment I went down on her. If I'd known, I would have finished the job to make her come so hard.

When she regained her confidence, she looked me in the eyes once more.

That was the first climax I'd ever given her. I'd been saving it until we fucked, but since that might not happen for another month, I'd had to improvise. Training a virgin was something I'd never been interested in, but now that I was doing it, I actually liked it. It wasn't just about popping her cherry and walking away.

Now it was about earning it.

She finally said something. "That was nice…"

My hand moved into her hair and pulled it out of her face. "Something to look forward to. The real thing will be much better."

"I have a hard time believing that…"

"Then take my word for it." My hands moved to her ass, and I gripped her cheeks with my massive fingers. "Here's another lesson for you. Never leave your partner hanging. And right now, I'm so hard I could explode—especially after watching you come like that."

Her fingers played with my hair, and she smiled at me. "What did you have in mind?"

Cherry Popper

"You give damn good head…I'll say that much."

She lowered her hands from my body and slowly slid to the floor, getting on her knees in between my thighs.

It was the first blow job I'd ever received in my penthouse, right in the living room in front of the TV.

"That act will be hard to follow." She grabbed my shaft and pointed my dick toward the ceiling. "But I can try."

12

Monroe

It was the first time I checked the mail and received something besides bills and spam.

I received a letter from the bank. It said that my two student loans had been closed.

Closed?

The new balance reflected zero dollars.

Zero dollars?

My loans had been paid off?

Well, I didn't do that. So who did?

One name came to mind—Slate.

I sat on the couch and called him. Now that I had his number, I didn't have to stop by his office every time I wanted to talk to him. And I didn't have to show up on his doorstep either. It rang a few times before he answered.

"Hey, sweetheart." His voice sounded deeper on the phone. Masculine and authoritative, he could be intimidating with just simple words. Without his beautiful package visible, he was just a powerful voice over the line. "Just finished my workout. What are you doing?"

"Just finished working out?" I asked. "Are you sure you didn't drop by the bank today?"

After a long pause of silence, he chuckled. "Got the letter in the mail, huh?"

"Yes. Which means you paid it off a week ago."

"More like four days ago...but pretty close."

I gripped the letter in my hand, feeling furious rather than relieved. "Why would you do that?"

"You can't figure it out?"

"Uh, no. I know you wouldn't just give me the money, so what's your angle?"

"It's simple. I've paid off your student loans so you can see how nice it is to keep more of your check. That way you'll be more motivated to keep your promise. You have the money...now you have to pay for it."

"Wow, that was a dick move."

"Really?" he asked. "I thought it was generous."

"Not generous at all. Look, I told you I'm not ready—"

"And I will wait until you are," he said calmly. "But I'm not going to let you keep teasing me. You've done it twice now—not gonna happen again. Now you have to uphold your end of the bargain. When you choose to do that is up to you."

I squeezed the letter in my hand, my rage slowly slipping away. I wanted to stay mad at him, but since the financial burden had officially been lifted off my shoulders, it was difficult not to feel a sense of hope. Knowing I wouldn't have to make those payments that month

Cherry Popper

drastically changed my life. I could actually afford food now. I could actually save a little bit of money every month. "Why do you want to fuck me so bad?"

"My reasons don't matter."

"Is it because of the chase? Is it because I'm the one thing you can't have?"

He took his time before he answered. "Your guess is as good as mine. Now, I'm surprised I still haven't heard a thank you."

"For what?"

"Making your life a million times easier."

"You did it to trap me."

"Maybe. But I've still given you all the control. You tell me when and where. I just have to sit and wait. Now that the financial stress is gone, perhaps you'll warm up to me. Perhaps you'll feel gratitude. As your money piles up in your bank account, you'll thank me for those numbers. And maybe your legs will open a little more…"

MY FAVORITE MOMENTS with him were the times we went to lunch.

There was no pressure at all. We were in public in broad daylight, so there was no affection of any kind, no expectations. To any onlooker, we seemed like two friends or colleagues getting lunch together—and nothing more.

We went to a pizzeria, and Slate ordered a salad and only ate one slice of pizza.

Now that I wouldn't be paying an extra fifteen hundred bucks a month in student loans, I didn't have to stuff myself every time we went out together. I could afford groceries, so I could pack a lunch every single day. Crackers would no longer be a part of my diet.

He wore a midnight black suit with a stunning blue tie. Anytime he wore dark colors, it always complemented his dark hair and eyes. He was the kind of man that constantly combated facial hair. It seemed like every time I saw him, he had a shadow along his jawline. He didn't have hair on his chest, and it didn't seem like he shaved it. His shiny watch on his wrist was never the same as the one he wore before. He changed it every day, so he must have had two dozen watches hidden in his closet somewhere.

Anytime a woman saw me with him, she probably hated me. A woman who could win over a man like him was naturally the most hated woman on the planet. I would probably feel the same way if I spotted him with someone else across the room. I would fantasize about the incredible sex they had on a nightly basis. I would imagine what it would be like to come home to him every day.

Too bad he wasn't the romantic type. All he cared about was fucking virgins—like it was a game.

I had no idea why he was like that.

"Does your brother do the same thing?"

He watched me as he finished chewing his bite. He took his time, as if he didn't care how long he made me wait. "Yes, he manages the hotels on the east—"

"I meant screwing virgins. Is he into that too?"

He stilled at the question, clearly not expecting it. "No. He has a fiancée."

"Does he know you do this?"

"I don't care what he does in the privacy of his bedroom, and I imagine that feeling is mutual."

"Does anyone know you do this?" I scarfed down three pieces of pizza and slurped my soda.

"Other than Max and the women, no."

"You've kept it a secret for five years?" I asked in surprise.

"Yes. There are some people who suspect what I do, but they don't have any evidence. Most women don't want the world to know I paid them to pop their cherry—or they just asked me to do it."

"So…how many women have you been with?"

"Virgins?" he asked.

"Yes."

His eyes shifted back and forth as he counted in his head. "Three a week times fifty-two weeks…times five…a lot."

I couldn't do that math in my head, but it was definitely a lot. "And you don't get tired of it?"

"No." He grabbed his fork and took another bite of his salad. "There are brothels all over the world that still offer these services. In ancient times, rich men paid a great deal for the experience. It's not that rare. And trust me, more men would do it if they could afford it. We're all dogs—some just do a better job of hiding it."

"I don't think all men are like that."

"Not all—but most. Good men are the ones who are honest about it."

"You can be honest about killing someone, but that doesn't make you a good person."

"Not the same thing, sweetheart." He finished his lunch then drank his water. "You must have fantasies too. Maybe you're not experienced enough to have them, but you do."

"But they're normal fantasies, like finding a good man who will treat me right, be faithful to me, and have a family with me. That's my fantasy—someone to grow old with. I don't want just a relationship or to be in love. I want loyalty—real loyalty."

"Loyalty is hard to find."

"Which is why it's so valuable."

He rested his elbows on the table as he looked at me. "I have a charity thing to go to on Saturday night. Would you like to be my date? It's black tie."

"Your date?" I asked in surprise. "Have you ever publicly had a date?"

"Not for over five years now. But I don't care what they print about me."

So he'd had a public date before that?

"My company gives a big donation to the police department. So we're one of the big sponsors of the night. There will be dinner, drinks, and I'll give a speech. Nothing too exciting."

"You'll give a speech?" I asked. "That sounds fun."

"Is that a yes?"

"No," I said. "I want to know why you're asking me first."

"Maybe seeing me give a speech in my best suit will turn you on."

Cherry Popper

"So that's the only thing you care about?" I asked with a laugh. "Any opportunity to get laid?"

He didn't show any shame when he gave his answer. "Yes. That's all I think about every time we're together. Our hot, sweaty bodies moving together on the sheets as I rock my big dick inside you over and over. I think about the drops of blood of your innocence staining my sheets. I picture the tears that fall down your cheeks. I imagine the moans you make when it starts to feel good…then I picture the screams when you come. Yes, sweetheart. That's my end game. I want you to let me have you." He blurted out his thoughts so fluidly, telling me exactly what was going on in that big brain of his. "So, will you come with me?"

Now, when he described our evening together, I didn't feel the same trepidation I once did. My thighs tightened under the table, and I remembered the way my palms felt against his hard chest. I couldn't forget the orgasm he gave me without even being inside me. When I pictured our naked bodies moving together, it turned me on. It didn't scare me, not the way it used to. I'd always felt a connection to him, that he wasn't just some stranger I hardly knew. I'd started to see him as something more, as someone who actually meant something to me. "Yes. I'll go with you."

13

Slate

To celebrate Coen's engagement, we had dinner at my mother's place.

My mother wasn't stupid. She was aware of the rift between us, the obvious tension that emerged any time we were breathing the same air. But she had no idea how bad our relationship really was, that we despised each other to our very cores. My mother's funeral would be the last time we got together for a family event. After that, we would live our lives separately—with the exception of work.

My mother had a beautiful penthouse with an enormous living room, a perfect location for her Christmas parties and charity events. She had two butlers, one for cleaning and one for cooking. Since she was unemployed, she probably didn't need the help, but she wanted the company.

We sat at the table together, the three of us along with Simone—the enormous ring on her finger.

Sometimes it bothered me that my mother never reprimanded Coen for how he betrayed me. I didn't need my mother to defend me, but I thought she would at least voice her disappointment. Like everything was perfectly fine, she pretended Simone and I had never been together.

"So, when's the wedding?" Mother cut into her pot roast, sitting gracefully like a queen with diamonds in her ears. She wore a white blouse with a string of pearls around her neck. She'd had plastic surgery, so her appearance was unnaturally youthful. But the doctor did great work because it wasn't obvious she'd had anything done to begin with.

"We haven't decided," Coen said, hardly looking at me across the table. "But something sooner rather than later."

"We want to start a family right away," Simone said, smiling at my mother and kissing her ass. "I'm not getting any younger."

"A family is the greatest thing you can have," my mother said before she sipped her wine. "It's the one thing I'm most grateful for."

I wasn't grateful for it, not when I had a shitty brother.

"We were considering doing something small," Simone said. "On the beach out in the Hamptons. Something before the summer is over."

I was about to drink from my glass, but I had to stop myself. "That's in a month."

"Yes." Simone looked at me, a smile plastered on her

face but evil in her eyes. "Fall is beautiful but unpredictable. And I already have my dress, so that's been taken care."

"Who gets a wedding dress before they're engaged?" I countered, knowing this was all just a ploy. She wanted to get married as soon as possible. The quicker she tied the knot, the less time my brother had to figure out he was making the biggest mistake of his life. "That seems desperate."

Coen glared at me. "Slate, come on. Can't you not be an asshole for one dinner?"

"You think I'm being an asshole?" My eyes moved to my brother, a man who didn't feel like family at all. "Oh, you haven't seen anything yet." I turned to my mother. "Coen doesn't want to sign a prenup. He wants Simone to share his half of the company. On top of that, Simone has already started barging into meetings like she has any right to be there."

Coen threw down his napkin. "Slate, what the fuck?" He was pissed I'd told our mother the truth—that he was being an idiot.

I held his gaze with no remorse. "Now I'm being an asshole." I turned back to our mother. "You need to talk some sense into your son. If Simone gets power over the company, it could jeopardize everything I've built—and it could affect your monthly allowance. You really want this gold digger to have access to something that doesn't belong to her?"

Simone looked like she wanted to scratch my eyes out, but she was powerless while my mother was there.

"She's not a gold digger," Coen snapped. "Stop calling her that—"

"Then sign the fucking prenup." I turned back to him. "You already backstabbed me once, and now you're going to do it again? This is our family's legacy. You're going to gamble it on pussy? Pussy I've already fucked—"

"Slate." My mom silenced me just by saying my name. "Enough."

The only reason I shut up was because she was my mother. If it were anyone else, I'd flipped the table by now.

Mother turned back to Coen. "Tonight is supposed to be a celebration, but your brother is right. We need to have a family discussion about how you handle this. If this were just your company, it wouldn't matter. But half of it belongs to your brother."

Coen looked like he wanted to strangle me.

Simone hid her disappointment, but not very well.

"But now isn't the time for such a crude discussion." Mother set down her utensils. "I hate to be rude, Coen, but could you and Simone excuse us for the evening? I'd like to speak to your brother alone."

"Gladly." Coen exited the room and took Simone with him. The butler escorted them to the door, and then they disappeared in the elevator.

When we were alone together, Mother sighed as she stared at me. "It's been five years, Slate. I thought this would be behind you."

"It's not about her." I stared straight ahead, where my brother had sat just minutes ago. There was a

Cherry Popper

picture hanging on the wall, the four of us gathered at Christmas time. "Couldn't care less about her. Coen stabbed me in the back. That's what I care about."

"He told me you were okay with it."

I turned back to her, my eyes wide open in shock. "He lied. I never said that."

"Really?" she asked, sighing in disappointment. "Oh, dear."

"Mother, Simone only wants him for his money. She came after me first, tried to pressure me into marriage. When I wouldn't cave, she started sleeping with him. She played me for a fool, and now she's doing the same to Coen. How can you not see it?"

"It doesn't matter if I can see it or not. Your brother is almost thirty. You think I have any hold over his actions?"

"No. But you have a lot of influence. I'm telling you, Simone only wants him for his cash."

"Then why has she been with him for five years?" she asked. "That's a long commitment."

"Because the company kept growing. Now we're valued at over a billion dollars. Of course she's going to stick around for a payout like that."

"People also change, Slate."

"Not that cunt."

"Slate." Her eyes narrowed.

I wouldn't apologize for what I said. "If he wants to marry her and give away half his wealth when she leaves him, that's fine with me. He deserves every bad thing that happens to him. But he can't risk the company."

"She would only own twenty-five percent."

"And that's too much. She would be making twenty-five percent of our profits every single day for the rest of our lives. She could be remarried, and that money would still be going to her. And if Coen dies while they're married, she would inherit the full fifty percent. And then I would have to deal with her…as an equal partner. So you need to get him to sign that prenup. I've already tried to persuade him."

"You have valid points, Slate."

"I know I do." It was difficult for me to be in the same room as Coen because it was impossible to forget what he did to me. Every time I looked at his face, I remembered the day I found out about the two of them, a picture in a tabloid of the two of them going into his penthouse together. Simone didn't owe me anything, but my brother owed me his complete loyalty. He threw away our brotherhood, our friendship, over a woman. There were millions of women in the city, and he could have any one he wanted—but he picked her. She was the only girlfriend I'd ever had—and he had to pick her.

"I'll try to talk to him."

"You better." My words meant nothing to him, but my mother's opinion still mattered.

"And you're sure your hatred has nothing to do with Simone?"

"Does it matter?" Whether she'd hurt me or not was beside the point. It was the betrayal that seared my veins, that made me stop believing in loyalty. I lost my best friend and my brother because he was a selfish idiot. "I hope she breaks his heart. I hope she ruins him.

I hope she makes him look like a fool for the entire world to see."

My mother placed her hand on mine. "I know you think you mean that…but we both know you don't."

14

Monroe

The back door opened, and a man helped me to my feet. We'd arrived at the entrance to the Plaza Hotel, Central Park directly behind us. I stepped to the side so Slate had plenty of room to get out of the car.

He was in a black tuxedo, looking even more handsome than he did in a suit. He'd shaved his jawline before he picked me up, so his face was as clean as it'd ever been. There were people gathered on the sidewalk, so Slate gave them slight nods in acknowledgment. He turned to me and circled his arm around my waist.

"What are you doing?" I asked.

He pulled me closer. "You're my date. And I'm treating you like my date."

"But people might think we're together."

He leaned down and kissed me softly on the mouth, not caring about the photographers and the onlookers. "Then let them think that." He brushed his lips across mine before he pulled away.

We entered the hotel then the ballroom where the event was held. The second we stepped inside, the white lights were bright in our eyes. To go along with the underwater theme, there were splashes of blue and gold. It was so elaborately decorated it seemed like we were at a celebrity's wedding rather than a charity event. "This is fancy…"

"They like to show off a bit." He grabbed two glasses of champagne from a tray and handed me one.

I let the bubbles drip down my throat and fizzle in my belly. "Even the champagne is fancy."

He pulled me away from the entryway so we wouldn't be crushed by the new arrivals. "You look beautiful, by the way." He looked me up and down, not caring if anyone saw the vulgar way he addressed my body. "I like that dress."

It was black and backless, stopping just inches above my crack. His fingertips gently moved over the bare skin, his hand warm. "I would assume so…since you bought it." I couldn't afford a dress appropriate for an evening like this, so he had one of his shoppers pick it up for me. I didn't want his charity, but I also didn't want to look terrible for the evening.

"Money well spent." A group of men approached him, ready to mingle. "This is gonna take a while, just so you know."

"I figured you were a popular guy."

Slate spent the next hour mingling with people he knew, police officers, judges, and other donors. The people he knew the best were from other successful companies, probably because they had more in common. He was charming, funny, and he always introduced me and kept me included in the conversation.

When it was time for dinner, Slate guided me to the reserved table close to the stage. There was already a couple sitting there, and judging by his nearly identical features, the other man was his brother. Slate pulled out the chair for me.

I sat down, feeling his brother eye me like I was the last thing he expected to see. There was a blond woman with him, and she also wore the same expression. It was innately unwelcoming, like I had no right to be at that table.

Slate sat beside me and rested his hand on my thigh under the table. He'd been perfectly polite the entire evening, making everyone laugh and introducing me to people I would never meet again. But now he didn't say a single word.

Neither did his brother.

The mutual hatred between them was palpable. I could feel it slide over my skin like a slithering snake.

The woman didn't make nice with me either, even though she and I should have nothing to do with this feud.

They served dinner, and still, there was no talking.

I felt awkward not introducing myself, so I went for it. "I'm Monroe…by the way."

Slate's brother gave me the same look of annoyance he gave his brother. "Coen." All I got was a one-word answer.

"I'm his fiancée, Simone," the blonde said beside him.

Then it returned to silence.

"THAT WAS the best steak I've ever had." I wiped my plate clean and not because I was starving. It was just that good. The sauce they poured over it, along with the grilled mushrooms, made it the most delicious meal ever.

"I'm glad you liked it."

"Did you like yours?"

"Yeah." He rested his arm over the back of my chair and leaned close to me, behaving like his brother wasn't just a few feet away from him.

"Are you nervous about your speech?"

"The only thing I'm nervous about is turning you on."

"Well, if you're that concerned about it, you could just take off your clothes. That works pretty well."

He brought his face close to mine, wearing a slight grin. "I turn you on?"

"Did my orgasm not make that clear?"

"You can make a woman come without turning her on."

"That makes no sense."

"You'll see what I mean, eventually. My goal is to make you so hot that you beg me to fuck you."

"You already do make me hot…"

"Not hot enough."

"Sleeping with a man for the first time isn't about hotness."

"But it'll definitely help." His hand moved into my hair, and he kept it out of my face as he looked at me, ignoring all the other people around us. His face was so close to mine that he could kiss me. Everyone else in the room could see the chemistry between us if they looked in our direction. All the women probably hated me, wondered what I had done to catch the focus of this beautiful man. If only they knew my secret…

The man on the stage kept talking about the work of the charity and how it benefited police officers who'd fallen in the line of duty. It was just background noise now that Slate looked at me like that.

I held his gaze and remembered how it felt to sit in his lap, to feel that impressive dick rub me to a climax.

He moved in and kissed me, his palm flat against my head as he kept me close. We were in public, but he didn't seem to care about the affection, kissing me in such a sexy way when everyone could watch.

That was when the man on stage announced Slate. "Slate Remington from Remington Resorts, our biggest donor, is here to share a few words. Let's welcome him to the stage." Applause sounded.

Slate finished the kiss instead of pulling back immediately. He let his lips linger a second longer, like he didn't care that the entire ballroom could see him kiss me. Then he left my embrace and buttoned his jacket as he took the stage.

I watched him move up the stairs, his body so thick and powerful. I started to clap and noticed the way his brother and his fiancée barely tapped their palms together. I had no idea what started their bad blood, but

I assumed Coen was the one responsible. I couldn't picture Slate doing anything to cause such tension. He was an asshole most of the time, but not unbearably so.

My eyes moved to the stage.

Slate took the podium like he was at his best when a crowd of people were staring at him. "Enough can't be said to thank the brave men and women who keep our streets safe day and night. This is the charity my brother and I support the most, and that's because it's very close to our hearts. I was sitting in my office a few years ago when an armed gunman stormed my floor."

I held my breath, not expecting this story.

"I'll save you the details because they don't matter. But I can assure you that moment wasn't my finest. They had my three young secretaries tied up in the corner and a gun in my face as he asked me to hand over all the assets in my bank account. He had the wire transfer set up and ready to go. Of course, I don't negotiate with terrorists, so I refused. If the New York City Police Department hadn't acted as quickly and efficiently as they did on that afternoon, I wouldn't be here today. The man had the barrel pointed right between my eyes—and it was only a matter of seconds before he pulled the trigger. Fortunately, that didn't happen. The officers arrested the man who held me at gunpoint and disarmed the situation with no lives lost. It was courageous, noble, and inspiring." He made his speech without any notes. Everything he said was completely from memory. "Unfortunately, that's not always the case. Thousands of officers every year lose their lives in the line of duty. This charity supports their loved ones when they're gone, provides for their spouses, and gives their children full-ride scholarships to any college they choose. It's a great program, and my brother and I will always be involved. Thank you to everyone for giving your donations this year. I've been told the program has raised more money this year than ever before. And that truly is amazing."

WHEN THE EVENING WAS OVER, we got into the back of his town car.

"My place or yours?" He sat near the window and looked at me with indifference, like it didn't matter if I wanted to go home or spend some time with him at his penthouse.

I had a bunch of questions for him. "Yours."

He told the driver where to go.

There was a lot of traffic that evening since it was a Saturday, so we sat in silence for the next twenty minutes until we arrived at his building. We took the elevator to the top then stepped inside his silent living room, no longer surrounded by the obnoxious sounds of traffic or mingling people.

He stripped off his jacket and tossed it over the back of the armchair. "Would you like a drink?"

"I've done enough drinking for the night."

He poured himself a scotch before he came back to me. "If your dress is still on, then you haven't." He took a drink then handed the glass to me.

I took a sip then licked my lips.

He took it back and eyed my mouth, like he wished he could have been the drop of liquor that was there just a moment ago.

"I have questions."

"I figured you would."

"That story is true?"

He set the glass on the end table then loosened his tie. He pulled it out of his collar and set it on top of his jacket. His fingers worked his shirt next, popping all the buttons and revealing his beautiful tanned skin. "Yes."

"That sounds traumatic."

"It was definitely unexpected. I keep a gun in my desk now."

"Hopefully, you never have to use it."

"I changed security measures after that happened." He peeled off the shirt and tossed it onto the chair. "Different rules, different cameras, different passcodes… stuff like that. This guy had managed to set up a wire transfer that couldn't be detected by the federal government…which was pretty impressive."

"Were you scared?" I asked.

"There was no time to be scared. All I could think about was the right moment to knock the gun out of his hand." When he was shirtless, he took another drink. "But enough of that." He stood in his slacks and his belt, his upper body so tight, lean, and muscular.

"Dinner with your brother was painfully awkward…"

He shook his head. "We aren't doing that either."

"Why not?"

"Because I don't want to." He held the glass in his hand and shook it slightly, making the ice cubes move.

I lifted the halter piece of my dress and pulled it over my neck so the dress fell to the ground. I wore no bra because that wasn't possible. I only wore a tiny black thong.

He slowly looked me up and down, taking in my tits the most. "You have the perfect body, you know that?" He set the empty glass down and walked toward me, his palms reaching for my boobs. He gripped them both and swiped his thumb across the nipples. "Tiny waist… big tits…perky ass…beautiful face." His eyes moved to mine again, their dark color drilling into mine.

"Answer my questions." I lowered his hands from my body.

Disappointment flooded his gaze. "That's mean."

"You know I like to tease you."

"You mean torture. You like to *torture* me." He glanced at my tits again before he stepped back and lowered himself onto the couch. "What do you want to know?"

"How long ago did that happen?"

"What?"

I moved close to him, my legs touching his knees. "The gunman."

"About three years ago."

"Have you ever seen a therapist about it?"

He scoffed. "No, sweetheart. I don't need a therapist. The memory of that day doesn't give me nightmares. It doesn't keep me up at night. It doesn't bother me at all." He relaxed against the back of the couch, his tight body still sexy despite his posture. His broad shoulders were wide and strong, and his powerful chest was like a brick wall.

"What happened with your brother?" I pushed down my thong and pulled it over my long legs until it turned into a pile at my feet.

He stared right at my pussy. "I don't like to think about my brother when my dick is rock-hard."

"This seems to be the only way I can get you to talk." I moved into his lap and straddled his hips, feeling his hard dick underneath me. His slacks kept his dick contained, but the outline couldn't be denied.

"I talk all the time."

"About serious stuff."

"We're just friends, right? Do we really need to talk about serious stuff?"

"I think we do when we have dinner with your brother and you don't say a single word to each other." I planted my hands against his chest, feeling how warm and hard he was. I could feel his rock-hard length underneath me, so thick it seemed like his slacks couldn't contain him.

He rested his head against the back of the couch and sighed. "It's not a good story."

"I figured." My hands glided to his shoulders. "Now, tell me."

"Alright." His hands rested on my hips as he looked me in the eye. "That woman he was with is his fiancée."

"Yeah, she mentioned that at dinner."

"Well, five years ago, before she was his fiancée…she was my girlfriend."

Cherry Popper

Since I couldn't picture Slate in a relationship at all, I couldn't believe what he said. All he did was pay to fuck virgins, but prior to that, there was a single woman in his bed. "Really? You and her?"

He nodded. "We were together for a few months. I wouldn't say it was serious, but we were exclusive. Then she started putting on the pressure for marriage. I thought that was strange because we'd only been together for six months. I told her I wasn't in that headspace at all, that marriage didn't interest me. Shortly after that, I caught her cheating on me—with Coen."

I gasped at the betrayal. "Oh my god..."

"I wasn't angry with her, even though what she did was wrong. I was livid with him because he's my brother...and his actions were wrong on so many levels. On top of that, we were close. We weren't just brothers...but friends. I confronted him about it, and he said it'd been going on for a while. I might have been able to let it go if she'd disappeared and we'd moved on from it, but he's been dating her ever since. Now they're getting married. He basically chose her over his own brother...and I've never been able to get over that." His eyes drifted down to my thighs, while he rubbed his thumb against my hip. "My hatred and resentment have only grown. Now he wants to marry her without a prenup, and that directly affects me. She wants to be part of the company when she has no business doing anything."

"She sounds like a gold digger."

He nodded. "That's exactly what she is. When she didn't get what she wanted from me, she went to him. Unfortunately, my brother is too stupid to see it. She'll own half of his shares, and when they divorce, she'll be a legal shareholder in the company. She'll get enormous checks for the rest of her life—and make my life a living hell."

"I can't believe your brother is so naïve."

He shrugged. "Pussy does strange things to men sometimes."

"Now it all makes sense…" I expected their disagreement to be something small that was blown out of proportion, or maybe a disagreement over money or company choices. I never expected a betrayal of this magnitude. "He's an asshole. A real asshole."

"I think so too. Not that this really matters, but…she was the girl I lost my virginity to."

"Then you've known her for a long time."

"On and off throughout the years."

"Does Coen know that?"

He nodded. "He knows everything. I used to tell him everything. There were times when we would go out to the bars and women would make passes at me, but I never did anything since Simone was in my life. But during that exact time period, Coen was sleeping with her. It's memories like that that make me despise him. He didn't even have the balls to tell me himself."

"No, he didn't have the loyalty to say no to begin with." This story was worse than the first one. Family wasn't supposed to betray each other like that. Brothers weren't supposed to be assholes to each other.

"If she and I'd broken up, and then he told me he liked her, I wouldn't have stood in their way. Like I said, it was never about her. I was never heartbroken over the thing she did. But the way everything unfolded…just made me hate him."

I didn't want to encourage that hatred, but I couldn't blame him for feeling that way. What Coen did was wrong, wrong on so many levels. It was unforgivable. And now it might affect their company. "Why is your brother so stupid?"

"I have no idea."

"So after Simone left, you started doing this…?"

"Yes." He lifted his gaze and looked me in the eye. "Simone was the only relationship I ever had, but it taught me that relationships aren't real. People can't be trusted. She only wanted me for my money, and then my own brother stabbed me in the back without thinking twice about it. I wanted to have my fantasy without risking anything. So…now I pay for sex. It's easier this way."

I couldn't tear him down for his reasoning, but his perspective was heartbreaking—and wrong. "Not all people are like that, Slate. Not all women would betray you. And not all men would be so disloyal. I know those people hurt you—"

"They both turned me into a fool. When the media picked up the story, I looked like some loser who couldn't keep a woman." He spoke without emotion, speaking of the past like it didn't bother him anymore. "This way, there's no way a woman can get to me at all. If she's a virgin, I'll fuck her. But that's it. I just wish I could get my brother out of the company."

"Could you buy him out?"

Slate shook his head. "He might be stupid, but he

would never be dumb enough to take that deal. The company is too lucrative. If we sold it to a third-party buyer, that would be different. But selling his half to me isn't the smart move."

"What if you sold your half to him?"

He sighed. "I've thought of that before. But I put in a lot of effort to make that company great. Frankly, I did a lot more work than he ever did. It would suck to give that up when he doesn't deserve it."

"Yeah…"

"So now I'm stuck with both of them. When my mother passes away, I'll never spend another holiday or celebration with him. We'll just see each other when we have to at work—nothing more."

"That's so sad…that a woman destroyed you like this." If she really cared about either one of them, she wouldn't have done that. She wouldn't have gotten in between two brothers and forced them apart. It was selfish and cold.

"I always thought money would come between us…not pussy."

I rubbed his chest and felt his cock soften underneath me as the arousal disappeared. His story was heartbreaking, enough to make anyone depressed. "I'm sorry. That must be so hard…"

"There are good days and bad days. But I think I hate my brother…" He shook his head. "My mother always told me that hate is too strong for people to feel. It has no place in our vocabulary. It has no place in our hearts. But I do…I hate him."

I rubbed his chest then his shoulders. "You know, if

you hate someone, that's usually because that person had a piece of you, a piece of your heart. They meant something to you, which is why they were able to hurt you in the first place. So, if you hate someone…that could be because you also love them."

"Not in this case. People hate people all the time, and there's no love underneath it. I think that's an ignorant thing to say."

"Okay, it's not true in all cases. But in situations like this…you're upset because he's your brother. You love him—"

"*Loved* him," he corrected. "He means nothing to me now. And he deserves every bad thing that's coming his way. Simone will rip out his heart, humiliate him in front of the entire world, and then castrate him. A part of me wants this to happen, just so he can suffer and tell me I was right." There was no shame in his eyes. "You can think less of me all you want. But people don't appreciate forgiveness or kindness. They only understand cruelty. That's the only thing that ever sticks with them." He gently moved me off his lap so he could stand. "I think you should go. I'll have my driver take you home."

"What if I want to stay?" I wanted to keep talking to him, to soothe the aches and scars all over his heart.

He grabbed my dress and panties and tossed them at me. "I don't care. I want you to go. So, go."

15

Slate

Anytime my thoughts lingered on my brother and Simone, it brought out the bitterness in me.

It made me want to be alone, to sit in my silent apartment and pretend I was the only person left on the planet. Perhaps if I didn't have to work with my brother on a regular basis, I could actually let this go. If he moved across the country and started a whole new life, I would never have to think about him again.

But now I had to look at him on a regular basis—that whore on his arm.

Monroe was only trying to make me feel better, but her comfort annoyed me. I shouldn't have asked her to leave, not if I wanted to get laid, but I was in too much of a bad mood. Even if she were finally ready to put out, I would have turned her down.

Days passed, and I went to work like usual, enjoying the parts of my job that had no interaction with my brother or his tramp. He was in the building often, but his office was on a different floor, and we never bumped into each other in the lobby. There were two sets of elevators on opposite sides of the building. He always used one, while I used the other.

Now that I knew Coen would marry her at the end of summer, I dreaded the passing of time. With every new day, his nuptials came closer. If that prenup were signed, I wouldn't care about his mistakes.

I hated knowing my brother's actions had a hold on me in some way. I didn't want anyone to have power over me in any instance. When they did stupid shit, it directly affected me. The company had been reinvented with my blood, sweat, and tears, but depending on how shitty things got, I might have to sell my portion and start my own company.

It would be nice to run him out of business.

The thought made me smile.

Even though my mom would be pissed.

I sat at my desk and watched my phone ring. Max's name appeared on the screen. I picked it up and took his call. "Max."

"Slate, what's the deal? I've got a line of beautiful women ready for you, but you aren't taking the bait. They keep asking when this is gonna happen, and I'm running out of excuses."

I had every right to continue my previous ways. Monroe was just another woman I bought, but I had to wait until I got to use her. In the meantime, I should live my life normally, satisfy myself with my specific urges.

But for some reason, I didn't want to.

My mind was so laser-focused on Monroe that another woman didn't seem appealing. Her cherry was the only one I wanted to pop. Once I had my way with her, my conquest would be finished, and my interest would evaporate. Then I would revert to my previous behavior since Monroe would no longer be on my mind. But for now, fucking another virgin didn't feel right, not when I would wish she were Monroe the entire time. "Let's put all of that on hold for the moment."

"What?" Max asked blankly. "The entire operation?"

"Yes."

"Everything alright? We've been doing this five years, and now you just stop? Something seems off."

"I'm just taking a break. Don't worry about it."

"So what do I tell the girls? Your shop is closed for the next month?"

A month should be plenty of time. Monroe had to crack before then. "Yes, we'll resume in a month."

"Alright…but you can't expect these girls to stay virgins forever."

They were all beautiful and desirable. Men on the streets could sniff them out like wolves. They wanted a piece of the action, to conquer virgin territory. But for every woman who lost their cherry to someone else, another one emerged. And their attributes didn't seem important in comparison to Monroe's. "A month, Max." I hung up and tossed the phone on the table.

Jillian spoke to me through the intercom. "Sir, I have

Simone here to see you..." Everyone in the building gossiped, so they all knew about the bad blood with my brother. They all knew Simone and I used to fuck before she started fucking my brother.

I couldn't believe that tramp had the audacity to come to my office. This was the beginning of the nightmare, the exact bullshit I wanted to avoid. Just because she was marrying Coen didn't make her an executive of this company, but Coen didn't have the balls to straighten her out. "Send her in."

Jillian escorted Simone into my office before she walked out quickly, trying to get away from the drama about to unfold.

Simone stepped inside my glass office, wearing a black dress with heels and a gold necklace. She had short blond hair, practically a bob. Her hair used to be longer when we were together. I wasn't a fan of short hair, regardless of how pretty the woman might be. She had a yellow folder in her hand, like she had data to share with me.

I could hardly look at her without hating her more. She was the evil wedge between my brother and me, the family-wrecker. She was so greedy that she didn't care how it destroyed our family. I didn't feel bad for Coen because he deserved this, but at the same time, I pitied him. She had a knife in his back, and she twisted it to manipulate him. Now he was at her mercy, unaware of all the blood he was losing. "You have no business on my property. All I have to do is call security, and they'll throw your ass out."

Cherry Popper

She didn't flinch at my hostility. She was too focused on her goal to let my anger defuse her determination. "Half of this building will be mine soon enough. Good luck getting me thrown out then."

I'd never wanted to hit a woman in my life, but now I felt the urge—the strong urge. I wanted to grab her by the neck and slam her head into the glass wall. Maybe a little damage would put her head on straight. "You aren't getting half of this place. I'll make sure of that."

"Even if you do, it'll still be mine when we're married. So unless you're thinking of killing me, you're screwed."

"Not the worst idea I've ever heard…" I stayed in my chair and kept my desk between us because the surge of violence was too strong. She probably wanted me to hit her, just so she could sue me and come after every penny I had.

She smiled at the threat. "I'm here to make a deal with you."

"I don't make deals with the devil."

"You should." She crossed her arms over her chest, still holding the folder. "Because he's the most powerful man in the universe."

"I think you're forgetting someone…"

"He's too weak, too forgiving, to see what's coming."

Wow, this woman really was evil. What the hell did my brother see in her? When we were together, her true desires were muffled. She hadn't emerged as the slithering snake just yet. But now, she wore her evilness like a billboard.

"Here's my offer." She came closer to my desk, her thighs touching the wood. "Stay out of my way, and I'll make this a pleasant working environment. I won't interfere with your business or change anything. You won't even have to see me. But make my life difficult…and I'll make yours a living hell."

"You haven't done that already?"

She didn't crack a smile. "You've already done some pretty shitty things, and nothing came from it. You're running out of options to make this stop. I suggest you take my deal."

"I don't negotiate with terrorists."

Her blue eyes narrowed with ferocity, and I couldn't believe I ever looked into those eyes when I fucked her.

"I'll just tell my brother and my mother about this conversation."

"Go ahead. Your mother might believe you, but she has no power to stop this. And Coen is far too loyal to me to listen to anything you have to say. All I have to do is turn everything around on you, and I'm safe."

My brother was absolutely pathetic. I was grateful I'd never been so stupid with Simone. I was grateful I had a man's sac instead of the boy's balls he carried. "You'll be found out eventually. Secrets and lies don't stay buried for long."

"And I don't expect them to. They just need to stay buried for another month—until I get what I want."

Cherry Popper

A FEW HOURS LATER, I made the rare trip to his office.

He was a few floors below me, having an office as spacious as mine. He had three secretaries too, all tall and pretty.

I wondered how Simone felt about that.

I didn't bother checking in with the girls, and they didn't stop me either.

They would be stupid to try.

He was alone in his office, so I opened the door and invited myself inside.

The second he looked up from his laptop, he looked pissed to see me. His eyes narrowed automatically and his jaw clenched, like he wanted nothing more than to punch me.

How ironic. The feeling was mutual.

"What the fuck do you want, Slate?" He sat back in his leather chair and spun a pen between his fingers.

"No need to be so hostile. It's not like I fucked your girlfriend behind your back." I would throw out that insult every chance I got, to remind him I was the one who should be angry—not him. I helped myself to the armchair facing his desk.

He sighed like he was sick of the jab. "It's been five years—let it go."

"Maybe I would if you apologized first." I never had gotten any remorse from him. Just hints of guilt when I confronted him about it—along with a ton of excuses.

Coen was still behind his desk, watching me without even breathing.

Sometimes, I wondered if he cared about what he did. It didn't seem like it most of the time.

"I am sorry," he said. "But apologizing isn't going to change anything. I'm in love with this woman, and I'm going to spend my life with her. Did you ever think that maybe she and I were supposed to be together, but she happened to meet you first? You really can't let that go and let your brother be happy?"

"Don't turn this into some bullshit fairy tale." Even if that nonsense was true, it didn't excuse what he did. "Take responsibility for what you did. You fucked my girlfriend behind my back—several times. Then you didn't even have the balls to tell me. I had to find out online—along with the rest of the world. So don't turn this into some stupid act of nobility. It would have been completely different if you'd handled it better. But you were a pussy—a pussy that fell for her stunt."

"It wasn't a stunt. She fell in love with me."

I rolled my eyes. "Right before she snuck around with you, she pressured me to marry her. No, it wasn't because she was in love with me. She wanted my company, and when she realized she wasn't going to get it, she went to the man who owns the other half."

"We've been together five years. That doesn't add up."

"Because she couldn't find a richer bachelor to cling on to. It's already become a public scandal, so if she made the moves on some other rich guy, he would know exactly what she was doing. You're her last hope of getting what she wants."

Cherry Popper

He shook his head. "You just can't stand the fact that she wants me instead of you."

It was so ridiculous that I couldn't stop myself from laughing. "Yeah…that's what it is." I was the one who'd turned down her marriage proposal. I was the one who'd stopped her from using me like a puppet.

"If we're done here, you should go." He turned back to his laptop.

I hadn't even addressed the actual reason I came for a visit. "Coen, we really need to talk about this. This is a problem that's not going to go away."

"Simone isn't the problem." He looked up to meet my gaze. "You're the problem."

"No. She came to my office a few hours ago and told me to stay out of her way. If I complied, she wouldn't interfere with my work. But if I opposed her…she would make my life a living hell once she acquires her part of the company." I wasn't the kind of man that lied or made shit up. I was always honest about everything, finding the truth to be masculine and noble. A real man wasn't afraid to tell the truth because he wasn't afraid of the consequences. My brother should know that since we grew up together.

"Why would she storm into your office and say that to you? It sounds like she's putting herself at risk."

"I have it on video if you want to see it."

He stilled at the revelation. "You have proof, then?"

"I have evidence that she was in my office and we had an intense conversation. But I don't have the audio." I didn't want to record myself talking to Max about the next virgin I would fuck at my hotel.

"Her coming to your office isn't evidence enough."

"Then why was she there?" I snapped. "Why is she coming to my office without your knowledge?"

"I don't know. I'll ask her."

"Or you could just listen to your brother…" The very man who was threatened by that psychopath.

My brother had his head shoved so far up his ass that he couldn't think straight—at all. "You need to drop this, Slate."

Now I couldn't feel bad for him. "I know I shouldn't even bother…but I don't want you to be humiliated, heartbroken, and scarred by this woman. She doesn't give a damn about you. She only wants you for your money, Coen. I'm telling you, you're making the biggest mistake of your life."

He kept the same bored look on his face. "You don't know what you're talking about, Slate. I've been with this woman for the last five years. I think I know her better than you do."

"Maybe," I said, losing interest in this ridiculous argument. "But this is what I know for sure. Once a cheater, always a cheater. She stabbed me in the back—with my own brother. Imagine what else she's capable of."

My brother was silenced by that last statement. He stared at me with the same derision in his eyes, but he didn't try to defend her actions.

I rose from the chair, knowing this was futile. I did my best to steer him in the right direction, to tell him how manipulative Simone really was, but he refused to believe me. If he wanted to live in ignorance, then I couldn't fix that. "I really hope you see the light, Coen. For your own sake."

I STEPPED out of the shower after my workout and quickly fixed my hair with my towel around my waist. It'd been five days since I'd spoken to Monroe, and I'd been too irritated to reach out to her. My week had been too shitty for company.

I turned on the music in my sound system while I shaved, and that was when my phone started to ring.

It was Monroe.

I quickly finished the last area on my face, turned off the music, and then put her on speakerphone. "Hey."

"Hey." Her feminine voice echoed off the walls of my bathroom, her trepidation audible in her tone. "How are you?"

I rinsed my face then patted it dry with a towel. "I just got back from the gym and took a shower."

"Ooh…does that mean you're naked right now?" she asked, flirtatious.

I saw my smile in the reflection. "I've got a towel around my waist."

"Ooh…sexy."

I chuckled before I patted the aftershave on my cheeks.

"But I asked how you are. Not what you're doing."

I ran my fingers through my hair as I adjusted it then pulled the towel off my hips. "It's been a shitty week. I'll leave it at that."

"Would a blow job help?" she asked, a smile in her voice.

"It wouldn't hurt." But a good fuck would be better.

"Well, can I take you to dinner?" she asked. "Then maybe we can head to your place for dessert?"

I was still pissed about the conversation I'd had with my brother, so my mood was sour like an old lemon. I wanted to stay in my cave and drink until I went to sleep, but she managed to wear me down with her pretty voice and playful banter. "I'll make a compromise with you."

"Just dessert?" she teased.

"How about I take you to dinner instead?"

"I can afford it, Slate. Well…now I can."

"That's not why." I didn't ever want her to pay for anything. A woman like her shouldn't pick up the tab. She deserved to be pampered, to be taken care of. Just because I paid her student loans didn't mean she owed me anything. Well…except her virginity. "I want to take care of you."

"You know, for being an asshole…you can be pretty sweet."

"I'm only sweet to you. Trust me on that."

MY DRIVER PICKED her up and drove us to the restaurant where we would be dining. She wore a red dress that had a strap over one shoulder and a deep cut up her thigh. It was a perfect color for her skin tone. With that deep brown hair, she looked stunning.

Cherry Popper

My bad mood disappeared the second I looked at her.

She leaned toward me over the middle seat and greeted me with a kiss. "Hey. You're more handsome than I remember."

I stared into her eyes as I kissed her, my hand tightening around her wrist. "I was just thinking the same thing."

"That you think you're handsome?" she teased as she rubbed her nose against mine. "I have to agree."

She made me melt even more, made the ice around my heart turn to water. Those innocent eyes and that soft smile made me forget all the bullshit in my life. It was easy to get lost in her, to pretend everything was alright. "Good answer."

We arrived at the Italian restaurant, and I was given a prime seat near the window in the corner. We approached the table, and I pulled out the chair for her before I sat across from her. I knew what kind of wine she liked, so I ordered a bottle for the table.

She picked up her menu and held herself perfectly straight. Her eyes scanned across the options, her lips pursed tight together like she couldn't decide what she wanted. "Everything looks so good…"

"Not as good as you." I would get the same thing I always did, something low in carbs and low in fat. It would be impossible to keep this trim figure if I ate the way she did. I wasn't sure how she kept her figure when she inhaled her food every time we were together.

She rolled her eyes but smiled at the same time. "What are you getting?"

"Probably the—"

"Don't you dare order a salad."

I set the menu down and felt the smile stretch across my face. "I like salads."

"But that's all I ever see you eat."

"Incorrect. I've invited you over for dinner—and I didn't make salad."

"Okay…that was the one instance," she said with a laugh. "But anytime we go out to lunch, that's what you order. How can a man your size stay so muscular if you don't eat enough?"

"I eat enough. I have a big breakfast every morning, a protein shake, and I have a good dinner."

"You just said you were going to get a salad."

"It's different at a restaurant." I grabbed my wine and took a drink. "They use so much oil and god knows what else."

She eyed my glass. "But you do drink like a real man, so I'll give you that."

"It's my one weakness. I don't have sweets—that's the trade-off."

"God, I could never give up sweets. You know those little Milano cookies?" She squeezed her fingers together, like she was gripping an imaginary cookie. "With the dark chocolate in between two pieces of shortbread? Oh my god…so good." Her eyes moved to the back of her head like she was having an orgasm.

I pictured that look on her face as I was deep inside her, my cock hitting her in the perfect spot to make her writhe in pleasure. The last thing she would think about were those chocolate cookies she just described.

She grabbed her glass and took another drink, like her little performance hadn't just made me think about fucking her. Whenever she took a bigger drink than she could handle, she always swiped her tongue across her bottom lip to catch the drops. She did the same thing when she finished swallowing my come.

Like always, she filled my dirty mind with dreams of sex.

The waitress came over and chased away my fantasies by asking for our orders.

We made our selections then passed the menus back. Now we were alone together, somewhat close to the other couples having dinner together after a long day at work. I stared at the woman across from me, the first lady I'd spent more than a night with since Simone. Being around her made me wonder what I saw in Simone in the first place. Simone was a beautiful blonde, but that was her only positive attribute. Monroe wasn't just beautiful, but smart, real, funny…and not obsessed with money. All she wanted was to be able to afford to live.

"What?" She drank her wine again, watching me stare at her.

I didn't realize how long it'd been since I last blinked. "Just thinking about work."

"Why did you have such a shitty day?" She propped her chin on her palm and looked at me. "Don't forget, we're friends. Friends tell each other these things."

"I don't know if I see you as a friend."

She pouted her lips. "That's a mean thing to say."

"You aren't supposed to want to fuck your friends."

"Who says so?" she countered. "Aren't people friends with benefits all the time?"

"But that's not what we are. I paid you for a service."

She shrugged. "Doesn't mean we can't be friends. When I first met you, I could barely tolerate you. But now, I actually like you…"

"But not enough to sleep with me."

"Yet…" She poured more wine into her glass before she took a drink. "But you're getting close."

"I am?" I leaned forward, enticed by this conversation. "How close?"

She shrugged. "I don't know. Just close."

We'd been doing this for several weeks now. I saw her often, taking her to lunch and dinner, spending time with her while being a gentleman. Even when I picked up women at bars and the gym, I never put in this amount of effort. Maybe one dinner at the most. Then she was on her back and taking my dick. I'd only take out a woman twice if I were trying to fuck her in the ass. "So, you think I'm sexy. You like me. And you think I'm kinda sweet. What more do you want?"

"I'm not sure. I guess I am running out of reasons."

"I agree." It'd been weeks since I last slept with someone. I was being satisfied in the meantime with good blow jobs, but that was nothing compared to pussy, especially virgin pussy. The one thing that really rocked me was popping a cherry. That was my biggest fetish, my biggest turn-on. And that was what I wanted to do with the woman across from me.

"Maybe I just like spending time with you…"

Cherry Popper

"Our time would be better spent if we were both naked."

"But once I sleep with you…will that be the end?" She held on to the stem of her glass and waited for me to answer, the hesitation on her face. Now she wasn't as playful as she'd been before. Now she was nervous, afraid of my answer.

"You know that's what I do. When I'm finished, we're finished." I took a shower then left the hotel room. I didn't even stay long enough to say goodbye. Just like a drive-thru fast-food joint, I got what I paid for then left.

She couldn't hide the sadness that crept into her expression. "And that's it? We would never speak to each other again?"

I shrugged. "I guess. I mean, if I ran into you somewhere, I wouldn't ignore you."

"But once you get what you want, you'll lose interest." She said it with finality, swirling her glass slightly as she looked into the contents.

The sadness on her face was impossible to ignore. It actually made me feel guilty, as if I'd misled her in some way. "My ambitions were perfectly clear, sweetheart." I made a few exceptions, like spending time with her until she was truly comfortable, but she wasn't more special than anyone else.

"I know…but I guess I'll miss you. I like spending time with you."

"I do too," I said automatically, not thinking twice about it.

"Then why don't we keep spending time together?" she asked, her voice growing quiet.

I held her gaze and tried to think of the right thing to say. Since I was her first lover, it wasn't surprising she'd developed an attachment to me. "I don't do relationships. You know that."

"You did one with Simone."

"And that was a mistake." Simone was the only relationship I'd ever had, and it wasn't real. It was just lies masked with sex. She humiliated me in front of the entire world. On top of that, she was the one who'd made me a man when I was fifteen. She'd been a leach for several decades.

"Not all women are like that, Slate."

"I'm sure they aren't." But I wasn't interested in finding out.

She stared at me with her chin still propped on her hand, looking at me with the same disappointment. "You know what? When someone hurts us, it sticks with us for a while. But we have to get over it. If we don't, then they continue to have this power over us. I know Simone hurt you, but the longer you keep this up, the longer she'll have you under her thumb. Don't let her do that to you."

Simone had no power over me now, nor had she ever. I was never heartbroken at her betrayal. I moved on like it never happened in the first place. "It's not because of her."

"It is because of her," she countered. "As soon as you broke up, you became the Cherry Popper, and you've been doing that ever since."

"Because I enjoy it—and stop analyzing me." I didn't appreciate a woman sitting across from me at dinner judging my decisions. "I'm a man with needs, and I will fulfill them however I want. It has nothing to do with that cunt."

"But it does," she said firmly. "You refuse to have a relationship because the only relationship you had ended badly."

"No." I kept my voice down even though I felt my anger rise. "It's not because of her. It's because of *him*."

She held on to her glass as her eyes changed, turning from serious to confused.

"People are greedy, selfish, and evil. My own brother stabbed me in the back while looking me in the eye. Simone was just an opportunistic parasite that found a better host. I don't have a lot of faith in people in general. So that's why I prefer things this way. I've been much happier ever since."

She let those words sink in before she opened her mouth to speak.

I cut her off before she had the chance. "Don't try to change who I am. Don't try to tell me I'm wrong. This is my life—and I will live it as I wish."

Monroe said nothing else. She stared me for a long time before she pulled the glass to her lips and took a drink. She licked the drops away and then turned her gaze out the window.

Now it was quiet. Tense. Uncomfortable.

I felt responsible for ruining the evening, but she shouldn't have pressed me so hard. She was asking me to be a different man when I didn't owe her anything.

She turned back to me and leaned forward, getting closer to me. "I wasn't trying to change who you are. I wasn't trying to say your way of life was wrong. But I was trying to say that you have options. You're a handsome, compassionate, and charming man...it would be easy for you to have the undying devotion of a woman. It would be easy for you to find a woman who would be loyal to you always. If that's what you wanted…"

Even if I wanted it, that didn't exist. I didn't trust anyone because no one was trustworthy. It was hard to believe a woman would want me for me, considering the nickname I'd earned. Any self-respecting woman would be disgusted by my actions, but my wallet somehow eradicated my crimes. "Simone came to my office and threatened me."

Her head tilted slightly as her eyes narrowed.

"Said she would make my life miserable if I didn't stay out of her way."

"So she basically admitted she's using your brother?"

I shrugged. "Why not? She already knows that I know what she's doing."

"That's still pretty ballsy...did you tell your brother?"

I nodded. "I did. But he didn't believe me…just as I expected."

She shook her head slightly. "What an idiot."

"When it comes to that woman, he can't see straight. She's brainwashed him. I tried to warn him for his own sake, but he doesn't want to listen to reason. So, I guess I'll stand by and watch his life fall apart."

"That woman is evil."

Never heard anything truer. "Yes." I shouldn't base my view of all people on Simone and Coen, but they were a sharp representation of reality. Once a beautiful woman seduced him, my brother turned into a back-bending bitch. And once Simone had the chance to be extremely rich, she stopped at nothing to get what she wanted. It was like an episode of *Game of Thrones*, but in modern times. For a man like me, I would never have the opportunity to meet a woman without my reputation accompanying me. She would always know I was rich. She would always know Simone humiliated me to the public. There was no possibility of meeting a woman on a blank canvas. I wasn't a regular man with a regular job. People knew exactly who I was before they even got the chance to know me.

"I hope your brother realizes the truth before it's too late."

"He won't." I'd watch Simone rip his life apart before she tried to commandeer the company. She was a pain in the ass, the biggest pain in the ass. She would rip my family apart until there was no possibility of reconciliation.

That was the worst aspect of all.

Monroe watched me with pity in her eyes, the sincerity obvious. I said she wasn't a friend, but the truth was, she was the only person I confided in. I told her about my life, even brought her to that charity dinner. And she seemed real with me, like she enjoyed my company because I was pleasant, not because of my money or the money I paid her. "You're a good man, Slate. Even after what Coen did to you, you tried to help him…again."

"No. I just don't want Simone to get her hands on my company."

"That's what you say…but I know that's not the main reason. I know you want to protect your brother even after he betrayed you. That's the sign of a real man, to put aside his own pain to help someone…even if they don't deserve it."

16

Monroe

After we finished dinner, we got into the back seat of the car. Our evening hadn't been as fun as I'd hoped it would be. Lately, it seemed like we were fighting rather than having a good time. Slate was in a bad mood, stressed about his brother and his future bride. When he told me he would never change, I felt the sadness in my heart.

I never considered a real relationship with him. It was something that didn't cross my mind. But the idea of never seeing him again after our night together… made me sad. He'd become an important person in my life, someone I spoke to on a daily basis. We had lunch together, dinner, and even went to special events together.

He was my friend…even if he didn't consider himself to be one.

I knew I didn't love him. How could I love someone

who called himself a Cherry Popper? But I knew I didn't want this to end.

"My place or yours?" he asked, looking out the window.

Our night had started off strong, but when I questioned his character, he quickly turned bitter. It cast a shadow over the evening that blocked out all the light. So I was surprised he asked the question, assuming he would just want to drop me off. "Your place."

He told his driver where to go.

I looked out the window and felt my heart start to palpitate. We'd been doing this for three weeks, and I still hadn't opened my legs. I was more comfortable with the idea, but now that I knew it would be our last night together, I didn't want to go through with it. I wanted to drag it out as long as possible. That wasn't fair to him because that was not what he paid for. He paid for a service—and I was supposed to provide that service. Now that I didn't want to lose him, that could only mean I was ready…and I should finally fulfill my end of the deal.

We arrived at his penthouse and stepped inside. I slipped off my heels right away and left them by the door. I'd worn my favorite dress because I wanted to impress him, and judging by the intense way he looked at me now, he was definitely impressed.

His hand moved over my bare shoulder, and his fingers squeezed me gently as he admired my bare skin. The backs of his fingers glided gently over my shoulder and to my neck, where he could feel the pulse in my vein. His eyes followed his fingertips, worshiping me in silence.

I turned my head toward his fingers and watched them caress me. I watched them move closer to me until the backs of his fingers met my mouth. They rested there, feeling my softness with his warmth.

I kissed his fingers, my eyes moving to his.

He watched me kiss him, watched me taste him in a way I'd never tasted a man before. "These lips are so perfect. So full. So soft. So sexy." He rubbed his thumb across my bottom lip as he looked me in the eye.

Whenever he touched me like that, I felt like nothing else mattered. There was no one else outside these walls. It was just the two of us in a deserted city. A man had never looked at me the way he did, with that possessive intensity. Did he look at all women that way? Until he got what he wanted? Would he only find me this desirable until he took my virginity? Then I would be damaged goods?

His hand moved into the back of my hair, and he gave it a gentle tug, making my chin angle toward the ceiling and exposing my neck.

He leaned in and kissed me, his strong mouth giving me the sexiest pleasure. He kissed me hard, his lips devouring me. His fingers tightened in my hair as he continued, as if he were eating me for dessert.

His hand released my hair and moved to the zipper at the back of my dress. He slowly pulled it down until the single strap over my shoulder fell to my arm. The rest of the dress came with it, slowly sliding until it fell to the floor.

He ended the kiss so he could look at my tits, see how hard my nipples were. He palmed one of them and gave it a good squeeze before he looked me in the eye again. His fingers moved to my nude thong, and he gently pushed it over my ass until it fell to my ankles. Fully clothed, he lifted me into the air and carried me to his bedroom down the hallway.

Maybe he expected tonight to be the night he would finally have me. He knew I was comfortable with him, that I still wanted him to be in my life once he popped my cherry. Maybe he knew if he pressured me, he would get what he wanted.

He laid me on the bed then stripped away his clothes. He got rid of his collared shirt, his slacks, and his belt. Piece by piece, he revealed himself until he was stripped down to nothing. His cock greeted me with the same enthusiasm as always, twitching in anticipation.

His heavy frame moved over the bed, and he approached me slowly, the mattress sinking every time his hand pressed into it.

My legs automatically opened for him, and I locked my ankles around his waist. Once I felt that strong body on top of mine, my reservations slipped away. My pussy ached because it was ready for the experience that would turn me into a woman. My thighs squeezed his hips, and I looked him in the eye as I felt his cock rub against my clit, stimulating me in the sexiest way possible.

He watched my expression as he gently ground against me, watched me feel him.

My hands gripped his arms, and I felt my nipples

harden to diamonds. My breathing became deep and heavy because I was nervous. I was about to give myself to this man, and I knew I wanted it. Even if I hadn't been paid, I wanted this man to be my first.

I brought his face close to mine, and I kissed him, my fingers moving into his short hair as I ground against his length. My thighs continued to squeeze him, and I moaned into his mouth the second our mouths were combined.

My clit was on fire from the pressure of his big dick. It wouldn't take much to make me come, not that it ever did.

He continued his purposeful embraces, his kisses turning more aggressive and passionate. He sucked my bottom lip then gave me his tongue, his cock throbbing against my clit.

My head was in the clouds, and all I could think about was sex, having that big dick inside me to take away my innocence. The other times he tried were met with resistance, but this time, I didn't feel any hesitation. "Slate…take my virginity."

His lips went immobile against mine, and I actually felt his cock twitch against me. He breathed hard through the pleasure, probably feeling a flush of heat down his spine. I'd just told him what he wanted to hear, and he was probably so hard it hurt.

I pulled away so I could look into his gaze, see the desire burning in his eyes. My fingers were still deep in his hair, and my pussy was wet from the way he rubbed against my clit. I didn't know how he would fit, but I was probably so wet that he could make it happen. When I looked back on this night, it wouldn't be with regret or shame. I wouldn't think about the money that had already eliminated my student loans. I would just think about him...the man who earned my trust.

He rubbed his nose against mine. "Sweetheart..."

I ground against him and felt my heart skip a beat. I could feel the audible arousal in his voice, hear the desire that tightened his spine.

"Not tonight." He moved off me and lay on his side beside me. His cock was still rock-hard like he wanted nothing more than to fuck me. But he turned me down, rejecting the one thing he wanted from me.

"Why?"

He separated my thighs with his hand then slipped two fingers inside me. "You deserve a perfect night. And tonight was far from perfect." He moved past my entrance and felt the moisture that pooled down my channel. "Besides, I need to break you in first." He leaned over me and kissed me, his mouth aggressive like it'd been before. His thumb moved to my clit, and he circled it as he fingered me.

The sting of rejection quickly faded away as he made my legs shake. I felt his large fingers press deep inside me, hitting my walls and making me loosen. His kisses drowned out my self-doubt and brought me to the edge of an orgasm. He moaned against my mouth as his fingers continued to explore me, to feel the virgin places that hadn't been explored before. He was a conqueror claiming a new land under his reign.

My nails sliced his skin as I felt the explosion between my legs. An orgasm as good as the last one he gave me rocked me from head to toe. My moans turned to pants, and I watched him look me in the eye as he enjoyed my performance. I felt my pussy slicken even more, more moisture dumping between my legs.

Instead of removing his fingers and expecting me to do something for him, he continued to finger me, just moving more slowly. His face hovered above mine, his chiseled jawline tight as he looked into my gaze. "I can't wait to fuck this pussy. So wet. So tight." He dug his fingers deeper inside, exploring me with throbbing digits.

"You could fuck it now…" He'd just satisfied me with his fingers, but I still wanted more.

He rubbed his nose against mine. "Don't tempt me, baby."

17

Slate

I COULD HAVE TAKEN HER.

I could have fucked her.

I could have finally had what I wanted.

But it didn't seem right. Our dinner had been tense and awkward. I snapped at her, and she got under my skin. She was different from the other women I bedded because this actually meant something to her. I wanted her to look back on the memory fondly, not with regret. I wanted her to look forward to sex, not be disturbed by her first time.

She was disappointed that our relationship would be over once I got what I wanted, but it was her mistake for assuming otherwise. She might be getting special treatment, but that was only because I wanted her so much. Once I finally popped her cherry, my obsession would die. I would be interested in the next virgin, hoping she would come and cry. Monroe would be a good memory but nothing more than that.

She wanted to stay friends—but I didn't have any friends.

I worked the next few days like everything was normal. As if my future sister-in-law wasn't trying to steal my company, and my brother wasn't the biggest idiot on the planet. When I was in my office working on my own projects, it was easy to pretend that I was alone—that I didn't have to share this company with anyone else.

I went home to my penthouse every night, worked out, and then drank booze while I watched TV. Sometimes my mind would turn to Monroe and I would fantasize about fucking her for the first time, but that didn't make me reach for the phone. I didn't want to pressure her into something she wasn't ready for. I wanted her to fuck me when she was absolutely certain.

That way, I could really enjoy it.

I paid her student loans, so now she owed me—whenever she decided to pay was up to her. I knew my reward was coming, and that made me patient. It also drastically improved her quality of life, putting that cash back in her pocket where it belonged. She had an even bigger loan looming over her shoulder, but that was much more bearable than having all of them combined.

My phone lit up with her name on the screen. I watched it ring for several seconds before I finally grabbed it and answered. "Hey, sweetheart." I leaned back against the couch and put my feet on the coffee table.

"I wish I had a nickname for you."

"You could always call me sir." I grinned because I knew she wouldn't like that one bit.

"How about pig?" she countered. "That's a lot more suitable."

I chuckled. "It is, but it's not very affectionate."

"Why would I want to be affectionate with a pig anyway?"

I grabbed my glass and took a drink. "What are you doing right now?"

"Sitting on my couch."

"You want to sit on my couch?"

"Are you inviting me over?"

"Sweetheart, you're always invited to come over."

"Really?" she asked. "Be careful…I might take you up on that offer. You always have food in the fridge, a bottle of wine, and your couch is comfy."

"What about me? Aren't I a perk?"

"When you aren't being grouchy," she teased. "I'll be there in fifteen minutes."

"You want my driver to pick you up?"

She chuckled then hung up.

Twenty minutes later, the elevator doors opened, and she stepped into my apartment. She wore cutoff jean shorts and a pink t-shirt, her brown hair straight. She set her purse on the table in the entryway then approached the couch. "Sweatpants and booze…had a long day?"

"Would you prefer me naked?"

"Actually, I would." She grabbed my glass from the table and took a drink before she scrunched her nose. "I don't know how you drink this stuff all the time. It's like liquid smoke." She took another drink then shook her head abruptly in disgust.

I took the glass back. "It tastes better on a woman's skin."

"I figured a woman would taste good on her own." She settled into the couch beside me, her hand immediately moving to my stomach as she came closer to me. Whenever we were alone together, she always showered me with this kind of affection, her fingers lightly clawing at my skin.

"She does. But sometimes she needs a little kick." My hand moved into the back of her hair, and I fingered the soft strands. I pictured myself yanking her head back while I rode her from behind. I'd popped a few cherries that way, and while I enjoyed it, I usually preferred to look into a woman's face as I watched her struggle to fuck a man for the first time.

She moved closer and placed her lips gently against mine, her perfume entering my nostrils at the same time. She kept her eyes open as she kissed me so softly, her lips like two pillows. Her hand pressed against my chest before she dragged her fingers down my sternum to my stomach. "Can I ask you something?"

"Anything."

She felt the grooves of muscle in my abs, her fingers catching the band of my sweatpants. She stared at my hard chest for a moment, like she was fantasizing about it being on top of her. "Have you been with anyone else since me…?" She didn't look me in the eye. As if she was trying to protect herself from my answer, she avoided the intimate gaze.

"No."

She lifted her chin and met my look, the surprise in her eyes. "Really?"

"Really." I was free to do whatever I wanted, but since I'd been obsessed with Monroe, other women became irrelevant.

"Why is that?" Her hand slid down to my thigh where she let it rest.

"I guess I prefer to conquer one woman at a time."

"But it's been almost a month."

"I guess you've hogged all of my attention." There was only one cherry I wanted to pop at the moment, and until I did that, I wouldn't be able to fantasize about anyone else. She was the only goal I had in mind.

Her fingers tightened on my thigh, and she took a deep breath, as if deep thoughts were passing through her mind. "So it's just you and me. It's been you and me all this time…" She didn't show happiness or disappointment. She seemed calm, at peace.

"I suppose."

"And you still think we'll go our separate ways once you get what you want?"

"Yes…that's how it works." I hoped she didn't misinterpret my monogamy. My celibacy had nothing to do with her. "I'm a goal-oriented person. I like to finish one task before I move on to the next. This project is incomplete, and until it is, I won't be moving on."

"But maybe it won't be complete after we're together."

That's what completed all of my arrangements. "I think so, sweetheart. Don't mistake my monogamy for anything more than it really is." I found Monroe alluring in special ways, because she had so many unique qualities. She was a woman who treasured her values. She was a woman so beautiful it hurt to look at her sometimes. And she didn't put up with shit—not even from me. Of course, I was obsessed with her. Any other man would be. But like all men, once I got what I wanted, my obsession died.

She pushed me back against the couch then straddled my hips, her jean shorts riding up until they hugged her ass cheeks. She pressed her hands against my chest and held her face close to mine, her light breaths falling on my lips. She used to be shy and reserved, but now she took the lead when she wanted me. She helped herself to my lap like it was hers to enjoy. She loved feeling my hard cock underneath her, pressing through my sweatpants and her shorts. Her hands snaked up my chest to my shoulders before she leaned in and kissed me.

Kissed me so softly.

Her pillowy lips rested against mine as her nails gently clawed me. Her warm breath fell on my face, heated my soft lips. Her eyes were closed as she held her mouth against mine, her kiss so soft, it felt like a rose petal. Then she kissed me harder, pulled my bottom lip into hers. She commandeered the kiss and gripped my shoulders for balance. Soon enough, our tongues swirled together, and our breathing became in sync. My hands moved to her hips, and I pressed my thumbs into her soft skin as her mouth continued to wreck mine. She slightly rocked against my length, applying pressure against her clit. Subtle moans escaped her mouth as she undulated over me. Her right hand moved into the back of my hair, and she ground a little harder, kissed me a little deeper.

She was one hell of a kisser.

It was my favorite thing about her, the way she kissed. She kissed like a real woman, a woman who wanted to please her man. Her fingers moved into my hair, and she brought our bodies closer together, until her tits were pressed right against my chest.

My hands gripped her ass through her shorts and squeezed the muscle. Her body was perfect, from her nectarine ass to her insanely tiny waist. With pale skin and slight freckles, she was a natural beauty.

And I was about to have her.

I knew she was ready. I knew these past four weeks had lowered her defenses and prepared her for what was to come. Now she didn't see me as some stranger, some random man who would haunt her nightmares. Now she saw me as her lover, as her friend. She was giving up her virtue to a man who'd earned it fairly.

Now I just had to take it.

I didn't want the kiss to end because it was so good, but I forced it to stop. I pulled my mouth away and stared at her hungry lips, seeing the desire still poised on her features. I maneuvered her to the couch then moved into the hallway, my fat dick so big, it stretched out the front of my sweatpants. I went into my bedroom and pulled out all the white candles I'd told my maid to buy for me. I set them up everywhere and lit each one until the bedroom glowed with flickering white light. Then I opened a bag of rose petals and spread them on my bed.

I'd never done anything like this in my entire life, but I wanted Monroe to have what she deserved. She wanted something meaningful and romantic—and I could give it to her.

When I turned around, she was standing in the doorway, her eyes reflecting the lights from all the candles. She looked at the rose petals on the bed before she turned those big eyes on me, surprise and joy bright in her look.

I'd never been romantic, but I could make an exception—for her.

I pulled off my sweatpants and boxers and stood in nothing but my skin. My dick was harder than it'd ever been, anxious to be inside that tight pussy I'd become acquainted with. I had been frustrated when she wouldn't open her legs in the beginning, but knowing I'd won her over made me enjoy it even more. I actually felt worthy of her—and not because I paid her.

I stopped in front of her then fingered the bottom of her cotton shirt. My eyes stayed on hers as I slowly pulled it over her head, catching a few strands of hair before they fell back down again.

Her eyes were fearless, like she wanted this as much as I did. She wasn't breathing hard with trepidation or stepping away with uncertainty. She held her stance in front of me, prepared for what would happen next. She had no idea how much it would hurt—or how good it would eventually feel. My hands reached behind her and quickly unclasped her bra so it would fall to the floor.

I stepped closer to her and found her lips with mine

as my fingers worked the top of her shorts. I kissed her with the same slowness she showed me, popping the button at the top and unzipping the crotch. They were already loose on her, so they slipped to the floor and landed with a dull thud.

I ended our kiss so I could take a peek at her panties. White and lacy, they were just as innocent as she was. They were the perfect choice for the night, and that told me she came over hoping that this would happen.

That I would take her virginity.

My fingers hooked into the straps along her hips, and I played with the material, wondering how wet her pussy had made the fabric. I pulled them down slowly, getting them over her curvy ass and down to her thighs. I lowered myself to my knees as I moved, and when I spotted them between her ankles, I saw the gleam from her arousal.

Her panties were soaked.

That should make fucking her a little easier.

I rose to my feet and gripped her hips, my thumbs slowly rising and outlining her rib cage. When I reached the bottom of her tits, I touched the firm curve of each one, feeling the warmth and softness. She had incredible tits, busty boobs that would be perfect for tit-fucking.

My hand moved into her hair again, and I kissed her as I guided her to the bed, my cock twitching in happiness now that I would come inside her, that I would pop her cherry and then fill her with my seed. I would mark my territory so every man who came after me would know the land had been conquered before.

I got her on her back with her head on the pillow.

Her legs immediately separated and locked around my waist, her enthusiasm the same as it was nights ago. Her hands moved up my chest, and she gave me a gentle squeeze with her legs, her lips slightly parted like she wanted to kiss me again.

She was the only woman I'd had in this bed, and staring down at her only made me realize how beautiful she was. From the slight freckles on her cheeks, to her full lips, to those big eyes…she was perfect. Her nipples were hard and pointed straight up, and her hair was in a sexy arrangement across the pillow.

Fuck, I couldn't wait to have her.

I opened my nightstand and pulled out the bottle of lube.

"What's that?" she asked, her hands still stroking my chest.

"Lube."

"You didn't use it last time."

"Because I didn't care about hurting you. Now I do." I poured it over my dick then smeared it everywhere with my hand. There was no doubt that she was slick everywhere, but getting my big dick inside would still be a challenge. When she fucked other men, she would realize just how extraordinary my size was. She would miss it and fantasize about it every time she fucked someone else.

When I was lubed up and ready to go, I anchored my arms behind her knees and got her into position, forcing her legs wide apart so she would be able to take me as comfortably as possible. I held myself over her with my lips just inches away. "Are you sure, sweet-

Cherry Popper

heart?" I wasn't even sure why I asked that question. If she said no, I would be devastated. I'd been wanting to fuck her for a month, so it was stupid to even put the idea in her head.

"Yes." She brought my lips to hers and kissed me, her knees close to her tits because she was folded into a half dome. Her fingers slid into my hair, and she kissed me hard, eager to feel that big dick move inside her.

She had no idea how much this was going to hurt. I pointed my head at her entrance and slowly slid inside, pushing past her lips and into the pool of moisture waiting for me. But that was as far as I got before her body tightened and resisted. My girth was too wide for her narrow opening, so I had to wait for her to relax, wait for her cunt to open like a flower.

Her lips faltered in their embrace before she kissed me again, her nails slightly clawing at me. The longer she kissed me, the more relaxed she became.

I took advantage of that and moved just a little farther. Now I only had an inch inside her—and I had a long way to go.

"You do have a big dick…" She spoke against my mouth as she breathed through the stretch.

"I know." I sank a little deeper, the lube my saving grace. My mouth was close to hers, but the more my crown felt the warm tightness between her legs, the less I could concentrate on two things at once. I could tell this was going to be amazing, the best I'd ever had. Her virgin pussy was crack, the most addictive drug in the world.

She started to breathe hard when she felt me stretch

her apart. Her hand slid to my arms, and she held on as the pain began to bother her. She couldn't kiss me because all she could focus on was the big dick trying to get inside her.

I sank a few more inches, tearing through her previously intact hymen. My dick got really hard every time I knew it was about to happen. It was just like cutting the ribbon outside a new building. It was a moment of finality, of accomplishment. I was making this innocent woman mine, so I could have a piece of her forever. "This is gonna hurt, sweetheart." I locked my eyes on hers and gave a slight thrust, finally claiming what I paid for.

She moaned loudly, her nails digging into my skin at the surprising level of pain. Her hips bucked as she breathed through the discomfort, her eyes slightly watery.

I imagined the drops of blood that surrounded my dick now, the blood of a virgin. Moments like this always made me want to come instantly, to explode on impact. But I kept sinking, slowly getting most of my dick inside her.

Now she was really uncomfortable. She gripped my arms with her legs spread wide open, breathing through the pain like she was giving birth.

She had an exceptionally small cunt. I'd fucked a lot of pussy, but never pussy like this. My cock throbbed inside her because everything was so good, especially the insane tightness. She wasn't just tight for a virgin. She was so tight that I didn't think it was possible for a woman to be any tighter.

Cherry Popper

"Fuck...this pussy." I had her pinned underneath me, contorted into an open position so I could take her. I would start off slow and give her time to adjust to me, time for her pussy to finally relax and enjoy me. And then I would fuck her hard like I wanted, driving both of us into an orgasm that made our toes curl.

I slowly started to move, to glide past the slickness and the blood and move in and out. I pulled back until my crown almost left her perfect cunt, and then I slid back deep inside, hitting her as far as her body would allow me.

Her hands pressed against my chest as she lay there and took it, took a dick much too big for her small pussy. She rocked with me slightly, her tits shaking back and forth, and she kept her lips slightly parted as she breathed deeply.

My entire body tightened in pleasure as my cock slid in and out. The lube kept me slick, but her pussy was wet enough that I didn't need it anymore. My biceps tightened as I moved my body forward and backward, sinking deep into her and pulling out. Out of my control, the moans started, beginning deep in my throat. Sex had never felt this good, had never felt more satisfying. Was it because of the woman? Or was it because of the wait?

The film of moisture in her eyes slowly grew into tears. A drop trickled down her left cheek, shining bright from the glow of the candles as it slid down her face toward her lips.

Fuck. My cock thickened even more inside her as the chills moved down my spine. Watching Monroe cry because of the size of my dick was so sexy. I was too big, and she was too small. "Sweetheart…"

More tears fell as her breathing became deeper and louder. Her nails dug into me every time my cock slid far inside her. She released a whimper of pain when I hit her good and deep, like my head was tapping against her cervix.

I didn't want to come because I wanted to do this for the rest of my life.

I wanted this to last as long as possible.

Because she was definitely the best I'd ever had.

"Do you want me to stop?" My hips kept thrusting because I couldn't stop. Monroe felt so incredible, better than any other woman. Her cherry was so sweet. I wanted to stay buried in her sweetness forever. I asked the question with sincerity, but my body couldn't stop until she actually asked me to.

More tears emerged from the corners of her eyes. "No…"

Thank god.

I widened her legs and moved deeper inside her, getting as close to my hilt as possible. I could feel the pressure from her walls, feel the tightness everywhere. She was squeezing me in every direction, like a boa that kept constricting. My hips wanted to move quicker, but I forced myself to stop, to give her more time to adjust to me. Not only was she a small woman, but her first time was with a big man. The least I could do was take it slow. "It'll start to feel good…eventually."

My hips moved a little quicker as my dick slid deep inside her. I felt her so intimately, felt the moisture flood across the surface of my crown. My ass tightened and my back muscles stiffened as I began to thrust more forcefully. I wanted to bridle my enthusiasm and keep it slow, but I couldn't help it.

This pussy did crazy things to me.

I started to move quicker and harder, making sure my body ground against her clit as I fucked her pussy the way I wanted. The first time for a woman was always difficult, but it was even more difficult with a man like me. I wanted to be gentle, but it felt too good to slow down. I wanted to make her come, but my dick might be a little too big for that.

I angled my neck down and kissed her as I continued to move inside her, tasting the salt of her tears on my tongue. My cock thickened and was on the verge of exploding. When I pictured all my come dripping out of her, it only made me want to come even more. My lips kept moving with hers, but when the sex was good, I easily lost my concentration.

I tilted my body farther and ground against her harder, doing my best to bring her to climax. If the pleasure became powerful, then it would mask the pain, and judging by the tears, she definitely had pain.

My kiss and the stimulation must have been enough to push her over the edge because her thighs squeezed me hard, exerting the kind of pressure only a python could reproduce. Her breath stopped in her lungs then she bucked uncontrollably, falling into an orgasm that made her scream in my face. The tears that stuck to her cheeks reflected the light of the candles, and her face had never looked more beautiful. In the midst of a screaming orgasm while trying to fight the pain, she was so sexy.

I could feel her tightness increase around my dick, feel the liquid arousal flood around my throbbing cock. A woman's pleasure was my fantasy, and making her come during her first time made me feel like a man. I paid for her virginity, but I wanted her to enjoy it too. I wanted her to have the best sex of her life—in the midst of the pain. I wanted her to compare every other man to me, to set her expectations high.

She breathed against my mouth as she finished. Her bucks slowly stopped, and her nails retracted from deep inside my skin. Once the climax passed, her pussy loosened. She took my dick a little easier, especially with all the moisture that flooded her channel.

I did my duty and made her come, so now it was my turn. But I still didn't want to release. I wanted to enjoy this as long as I could, to live in this moment forever. I could only pop a woman's cherry once. When this was over, Monroe wouldn't be a part of my life anymore. The thought made me sad, so I kept going, wanting to stretch this out as long as possible. I could make her come again, make her legs shake for me.

So that's what I did.

Now that she was looser, I fucked her harder than before, getting my dick deeper inside her. I didn't need to apply more lube because she was wet enough. But the longer I fucked her, the more I wanted to come.

Thankfully, she came again, a little weaker than last time, but still enough to soak my dick again.

Fuck, I couldn't keep it together now.

Her tears stopped now that she was used to it, now that my big dick had successfully stretched her wide apart. Her fingers dug into my hair, and she brought me close to her lips. "Come inside me…" She held my gaze with her lips slightly parted, looking like the sexiest woman who had ever said those words to me.

I was already on the verge of exploding, so those words gave me the push I didn't need. I'd spent most of my time with this woman, kissing her and touching her. Now I'd finally claimed her—and she was worth the wait. Now the explosive moment was about to happen. I was going to stuff her with my come and fill her completely.

After a few thrusts, I released, dropping everything I had with an aggressive grunt. The sensation started in my balls then quickly exploded up my shaft. It reached my tip then gave me the greatest sensation of pleasure I'd ever felt. I had to close my eyes because it felt so good. Another moan escaped my lips, and it was so guttural I hardly recognized my own voice. I shoved myself deep inside her because I wanted her to capture every drop, to feel my essence deep within her. My ass tightened as I finished, and the clouds of pleasure slowly faded away. I opened my eyes and looked at her, looked at the woman I'd conquered.

I bent my head down and kissed her, gave her a tender embrace I never gave anyone else. My hand moved into her hair, and I stayed between her legs as I treasured her, silently apologizing for the aggressive way I took her.

I slowly pulled out of her, careful not to spill any of

my seed, and then I lay beside her. The only lights in the room were the candles, so we lay on the rose petals while the wax slowly dripped. The city was visible outside the windows, and the bedroom was quiet with the exception of our deep breathing.

She moved close to me and hooked her arm around my waist, resting her face on my chest.

I was hot and sweaty, but I didn't push her away. I let her cuddle into me when no one else had that right. Normally, I would hop in the shower the second sex was finished, then leave the room, but I stayed by her side because there was nowhere for me to go.

I was too tired anyway.

I felt like a boulder fell on my body and crushed me into the floor. She knocked the wind out of me, made me breathless. With the others, I went about my day and continued like nothing happened. But with Monroe, I felt so weak that I couldn't move.

That I could just stay there forever.

18

Monroe

When I woke up the next morning, I was on his chest, sleeping like a cat trying to stay warm. His chest rose and fell slowly, practically lulling me back to sleep even though it was late in the morning.

I opened my eyes and looked across his bedroom, remembering everything that happened last night. I gave myself to him without reservation, my legs wide open so I could take all of him, his length and his girth. I cried because of the pain, cried because of the way he stretched me. It was a sensation I never could have anticipated. Sex was supposed to be the greatest sensation in the world, but my first time was a challenge.

It took a long time before it started to feel good, and even when it did, it still hurt the entire way through.

But it aroused Slate, watching me struggle to take his big dick. His eyes had a look of desire he'd never displayed before. His jaw tightened, and the sweat slicked across his chest with a sexy gleam. He tried to be gentle with me, but his body had other plans. His cock wanted more of me, couldn't help but hit me deep and hard.

That turned me on, watching that beautiful man enjoy me so much.

They said the first time would hurt no matter what, but I suspected it hurt more because Slate was so large. Would I have wanted him to be smaller? Probably not. I would just have to get used to him.

He stirred underneath me, opening his eyes and taking in the morning light. As if I was featherlight, he didn't notice I was on his chest until he started to move. He turned his face to mine and looked at me. "Morning."

"Morning." I leaned down and kissed him.

He kissed me back before he rolled me onto my back. "How's your girl? Sore?"

"A little."

He moved his head under the sheets and planted a soft kiss at my entrance.

I tensed at the contact, my eyes closing when I felt the softness of his lips against mine.

His head reemerged, and he looked down at me, a shadow of a beard growing along his jawline. "It'll feel better in a few days."

Not if he fucked me sooner than that.

"I need to take a shower and get to work." He left the bed and walked into the bathroom, his bare ass muscular and sexy. He rounded the corner and disappeared.

Cherry Popper

Once he was out of the room, I suddenly felt cold inside. I expected him to take me again before he started his day. I expected some kind of playful banter back and forth. It was the first time I'd slept over, and now I didn't want to leave this big bed. It was so comfortable, so warm.

I got out of bed and put on my clothes and looked at the time. I didn't realize how late it was, and unless I left right this minute and headed to my apartment to change, I would never make it before I was officially late for work.

I went into the bathroom and raised my voice over the falling water. "I've got to head to work. Otherwise, I'm going to be late." The steam rose from his large walk-in shower, and inside stood a muscular, naked man, rubbing soap across his beautiful skin.

"Alright." He rubbed the bar of soap across his chest then down his arms. "Bye, Monroe."

I didn't like the way he said bye. It was a word I'd never heard him explicitly use before. And he usually called me sweetheart to top it off. "Bye…"

———

THE FIRST FEW days were filled with bliss. Losing my virginity was a memory I would treasure forever, because it was with a man I adored. He had a kind heart that was hidden inside a rough exterior. Sometimes he was standoffish and unbearable, but underneath that ruggedness was always a man with good intentions.

He was my friend—my best friend.

But the days passed, and he never called.

He didn't text either.

He'd told me once the deed had been done, he would be gone. The second he popped my cherry, his obsession would disappear. I believed him in the beginning, but then I started to doubt his sincerity when he said he'd been celibate for this last month. He spent most of his free time with me, cooking me dinner and taking me out to fancy places. We began to have a real connection, and I believed he would want me more once he had me—but that didn't seem to be the case.

There had been lots of times when we hadn't spoken to each other for days on end. He got busy and I got busy. It was nothing to panic about. But when I didn't hear from him, the self-doubt started to rip me apart.

Had he forgotten me already?

Was I just another notch in his belt?

He'd told me this was nothing but a transaction, but I struggled to believe that. It felt like something more, from my end as well as his.

Or had I been wrong?

When a week passed, I stopped caring about the higher balance in my bank account. My life had become significantly easier, even with the burden of my mother's medical bill, but I was too sad to appreciate it.

Now I thought about the man who had disappeared.

The one who made me laugh, smile, and happy.

Had he forgotten about me already?

His prolonged silence should have been an affirmation that he wasn't interested in seeing me anymore, but

I didn't want to believe that. I wanted to believe there was more here, that we really had something. My attachment wasn't just because he was my first. It was much deeper than that.

I decided to call him from my couch in the living room.

It rang and rang…and rang.

Then went to voice mail.

I'd never heard his voice mail before.

I hung up without leaving a message and set the phone beside me, my stomach tied in knots like someone had just kicked me. I pulled my knees to my chest and rested my fingertips over my lips, reeling from the cold rejection. I sat in my apartment alone as I stared at the phone, offended he didn't even have the courtesy to take my call. He got what he wanted, and now he wanted nothing to do with me.

I knew I shouldn't be angry, not when he warned me this would happen.

But I was.

I was angry because I refused to believe this was what he really wanted. He'd never chased a woman as hard as he chased me. A single night was all he needed to be satisfied? I wasn't satisfied at all.

I wanted to call him again, but I refused to appear so clingy.

And if he didn't call me back…then my first impression of him was right.

He really was an asshole.

HE NEVER CALLED ME BACK.

It'd been almost two weeks since we last spoke.

I couldn't believe he felt so little for me that he wouldn't even return my phone call. We spent an entire month together, and I thought I'd earned more respect than that. I might have provided a service, but I also provided my friendship.

Even that meant nothing to him?

By the time I got off work, smoke was blowing out of my ears. I was hurt that I meant so little to him, that we had something real, but he didn't value it. After the way he'd been burned in the past, he was afraid to get close to anyone…but I wasn't just anyone. I expected him to put aside that fear and actually step up and be a man.

So I went to his penthouse.

Maybe it was wrong to show up on his doorstep unannounced, but this wouldn't have happened if he'd returned my phone call. I stepped into the elevator, and even though I knew the code, I pressed the intercom button to speak to him. "Slate, it's Monroe. I'm coming up."

He didn't speak back to me through the intercom, but he hit the button so the elevator would rise to the front of his penthouse.

The doors opened and revealed his living room, the glass of scotch on the coffee table while the TV showed a football game. He sat on the couch in just his sweatpants, his beard much thicker than the last time I saw him. He watched me with his brown eyes, slightly hostile but not overly unwelcome.

Now that we were face-to-face, my courage fizzled out like a can of soda that had been open too long. I stepped into his living room, dressed in the yellow sundress and jean jacket I wore to work that afternoon. Last time I was there, I had a great night with a great man. But now, he was just some stranger. I slowly approached the couch and noticed the way he didn't rise to greet me.

He didn't show me an ounce of affection.

Maybe I really did mean nothing to him.

He took another drink of his scotch and rose to his feet. "How can I help you, Monroe?" He stared at me with indifference, like I was insignificant to him. He stepped closer to me but kept his arms by his sides. Muscular and gorgeous, he was exactly the same as he'd been two weeks ago, but now he was ice cold.

"How can you help me?" I whispered back. "You could start by explaining why you never called me back."

"I'm not obligated to call you back."

I couldn't keep the shock off my face. The last time we were together, he kissed me between my legs then hopped in the shower. Now he behaved like that never happened. "What if I needed help?"

"Not my problem."

"Wow…you really are an asshole."

He didn't flinch at the insult. "Monroe, I told you what this was. I told you there was only one thing I wanted. When I got it, this would be over. I enjoyed the chase, but once I claimed my reward, that was it."

I refused to cry in front of him, to let him know how

much he hurt me. It took all my strength, but I managed to pull it off. I was able to bottle all my hurt deep inside until I finally left his penthouse. "We have something, Slate. We both know it."

"Friendship and lust."

"No, something more than that."

"Well, that feeling isn't mutual." His brown eyes were aflame like two burning fires.

"You hadn't been with anyone else—"

"You're reading too much into that. I like to focus on one woman at a time."

"And take them to dinner?" I asked incredulously. "Cook for them? Pay them double? That was out of the ordinary."

"But it doesn't mean anything," he said simply. "The more you resisted me, the more I wanted you. End of story."

"Have you been with anyone else since?" There was only one answer I wanted to hear. If he gave the one I didn't want, I'd struggle to keep my emotions together.

"That's none of your business."

"So, no." I couldn't keep the victory out of my voice. "Why are you fighting this?"

"I'm not fighting anything, Monroe. I don't want anything more to do with you."

I shook my head in disappointment. "I always thought you were a strong man, and strong men aren't afraid to say how they feel. You're running away like a damn pussy. I thought you were better than that."

His eyes narrowed with a hint of fire. "Get out, Monroe."

"You're really going to just throw us away?"

"We were never anything to throw away. I paid for your virginity, and that's the end of the relationship. Now, leave." He turned his back to me and grabbed the decanter of scotch. He refilled his glass and threw his head back and drank.

"Fine. If you want to sit here and drink all by yourself, then have a good time. If you want to give up on people and relationships, so be it. If you're too scared to actually live your life…then that's your problem. Don't expect me to wait around until you change your mind. Because I'm not the kind of woman that waits around for any man—including you."

AFTER SHEDDING a few tears during the walk, I ended up in a bar close to Slate's building. The place was fairly quiet because it was a Wednesday night. Friends sat together in booths, and couples shared a drink at the tables. I was one of the few people at the actual bar, but I didn't want company, so that was fine with me.

I ordered a scotch. It tasted like smoke and burned my throat, but I needed something stronger than wine. The extra cash in my account seemed tainted, so I wanted to piss it away on my sorrow. I'd sold myself to a man who never cared about me, and I was an idiot for thinking he ever did.

How could I be so naïve?

Maybe he was lying about his feelings now, but did it really matter if he was?

He refused to let himself want me.

It was just as bad as not caring.

I thought I'd just sold my virginity to him, but now I wondered if I'd sold my heart as well.

A man moved onto the stool beside me, a scotch in his hand. "You don't see beautiful women order scotch too often."

I turned to look at the man who joined me, a young and handsome guy in a suit. He seemed like a big shot like Slate because he had a fancy watch on his wrist, wore expensive cologne, and carried himself like he was important. "I don't usually drink scotch…only when I'm having a bad day."

"What kind of bad day are you having? Like…you just broke up with your boyfriend kind of bad day?" He leaned toward the counter and grinned.

"Is that how you hit on women?" The booze had already gotten to me. I was buzzed and less inhibited.

"It's how I figure out if they're taken…and I hope you aren't." He drank from his glass as he kept his blue eyes on me. He was a pretty man, leaner in musculature than Slate but handsome all the same.

"I'm not. And that's exactly why I'm drinking."

"Bad breakup, huh?" He turned on his stool so he faced me, the side of his body leaning against the counter.

"Not exactly. But pretty much."

"If you're here looking for a rebound, I'm totally available." If he weren't so handsome, he might come off a bit creepy. He was extremely forward, and maybe that was normal for a bar in Manhattan.

I wouldn't know; I didn't go out much. "If you're looking to get laid, you're wasting your time with me. You're a good-looking guy, so I'm sure you could pick up some other woman in here."

"You think I'm good-looking?" he asked, his grin stretching further.

When he smiled like that, he looked familiar. Like I'd seen somewhere before but couldn't place exactly where, his face resonated with me. It was unlikely that I'd ever met him, but maybe I'd seen him on the TV or a billboard. "I feel like I know you from somewhere... Have we met?"

"No. If I'd met you before, I would have remembered."

I turned on my stool and faced him, still unable to place him. "I'm Monroe, by the way."

"Beautiful name for a beautiful woman. I'm Wyatt." He drank from his glass. "So, you want to tell me what happened?"

"You actually want to hear it?" I asked in surprise. He should move on to someone else, a woman who would get on her back in thirty minutes or less. Listening to my problems would just put him to sleep.

"Absolutely." His hands came together as he prepared to listen. "Lay it on me. I'm a man, so maybe I can give you some advice."

"I don't think I need advice. This guy is just an asshole...nothing too cryptic."

"Ouch," he said with a cringe. "This guy hurt you good."

"I'm sure you can see the puffiness under my eyes…"

He shrugged. "Your beauty covers it up pretty well. So, what did this asshole do?"

"Well…" I felt weird telling him the truth, but then I also realized I would never see him again. I wasn't going home with him, so what was the harm? As long as I didn't confirm Slate's identity, it shouldn't matter. "You're probably going to judge me for this, but this man bought my virginity. In exchange for claiming my purity, he paid back my student loans. I only agreed to the arrangement because I was drowning in so much debt, and when it was time to do the deed…I chickened out. I wasn't ready for it. So we spent a month together, going out to dinner and being together so I would feel more comfortable. I developed feelings for him, and I thought he felt the same way. So…we did it. And the next morning, everything was over. He wanted nothing to do with me."

Wyatt could have called me a whore, but he didn't. A lot of people would think less of me for giving up my virtue for money, but I didn't care what they thought. I needed to do it to survive, to have some kind of future. Even though Slate hurt me, I would do it again in a heartbeat. Wyatt didn't have an overt reaction, his face exactly the same, like he was waiting for me to elaborate even more.

"I called him, and he never called me back. I confronted him at his place, and he was a completely different person…said he got what he wanted." I shook my head at the memory. "I know he's just scared to be

Cherry Popper

close with someone since he's been burned in the past. But I can't believe he's this pathetic. He should trust me, should know I'm nothing like the people who ripped him apart. So now I'm here...drinking my problems away." I grabbed my glass and took a drink.

Wyatt still didn't say anything, but he didn't look at me with judgmental eyes. "That's harsh."

"He told me that's what would happen...but it seemed like we were closer than that."

"A month is a long commitment for a man who can pay for any pussy he wants."

A month wasn't long enough for me. He'd just broken my heart and hurt me so deeply, but I still missed him...even after those tears cascaded down my face. "So, that's why I'm drinking alone...and I don't usually drink like this."

"No judgments," he said. "Can I ask you something?"

"Sure."

"How old are you?"

"Twenty-three."

"You were an old virgin."

"Yes, I've heard that before," I said. "I was just waiting for the right guy...but then my loans crushed me."

"How much are we talking here?" He finished his glass then ordered both of us another round.

"Almost $200,000."

Both of his eyes snapped wide open. "Two hundred thousand? Are you a doctor or something?"

"No...I wish." At least I would be making more

money. "I have a masters in marketing. I'm an executive at Cutie Clothes."

He nodded slowly. "That's why you recognize me."

"Excuse me?"

"I'm the CEO of Silk, the women's fashion line."

The second he said those words, everything clicked into place. "I knew I recognized you from somewhere…" I'd been comfortable with him just a minute ago, and now I was seriously intimidated. This man was a fashion icon, running a company that produced fashion gems that women dreamed of. Not only was he successful, he was brilliant. And I happened to bump into him at a bar on a Wednesday night.

"Don't start acting weird around me. This conversation has been delightful so far…until you realized who I was."

"I'm not being weird. I'm just…a big fan." I grabbed my glass but felt my hand shake as I gripped it. "Silk is an amazing company. The clothes, the fabric… I worked a second job one summer just so I could buy a pair of your heels."

"You flatter me," he said with a smile. "Looks like we have a lot in common. Cutie Clothes has some good stuff too."

"It's not Silk," I said with a laugh. "Your clothes are sophisticated and sexy without showing too much skin. The patterns are so subtle but so powerful. I love Cutie Clothes, don't get me wrong, but Silk is phenomenal." If I had more money, I would buy more clothes. Maybe it was a good thing I was poor.

Cherry Popper

The corner of his mouth rose in a smile. "What do you do in marketing?"

"I handle all the editorial placements, the billboards, and the digital ads we put everywhere. It doesn't sound like much, but those ads have to be updated every three days before they go stale. It's constant."

"No, I understand. It's the biggest job in the company. What's the point of making a great product if no one knows it exists? Or better yet, what's the point of having a company without having a brand? Very vital to the health of the business." He tapped his two fingers against his skull.

"So…what's your story?"

"Pardon?" he asked, having no idea what I was referring to.

"With your love life? Is there a douchebag woman out there who wronged you?"

"Not really," he said. "Nothing like what happened to you. I'm a serial monogamist, but my relationships don't last very long."

"Because you don't want them to?"

"No. They just don't. I'm not looking to settle down, but if I met the right woman, I would stick it out. But finding the right woman in Manhattan is impossible."

"There are seven million people who live here," I said with a laugh. "So how's that possible?"

"Well, most women know who I am, so they care more about my success than the man underneath the suit."

Slate told me the horror story about his brother, that

he had a backstabbing woman who only wanted to pick his pocket. "Yeah, I can see that. That's unfortunate. Maybe you should start dating in Iowa or something."

He chuckled. "That's quite a commute."

"But no one would know who you are."

"Probably not," he admitted, keeping his fingers wrapped around his glass. He watched me for a while, his blue eyes a lot kinder than Slate's brown ones. He wore a boyish smile as he spoke. "You want to have dinner with me sometime?"

"I don't live in Iowa."

He chuckled. "I'll make an exception."

"I just told you I sold my virginity for money. That's not a turn-off for you?"

"It was in the beginning, but when you told me how much you owed in student loans, I couldn't blame you. You'd be paying that back until the day you died."

I would pay back my mother's hospital bill until the day I died. "Yep…"

"So, no, I don't judge you. Your first time is usually a bad experience anyway, so you might as well get paid for it, right?"

It wasn't a bad experience. I had been hoping it would be the first of many experiences.

"So, is that a yes?"

My instinct was to say no. Just an hour ago, I showed up at Slate's apartment demanding an explanation for his coldness. He hurt me more than I realized, and turning my back on him was one of the hardest things I'd ever had to do. I felt like I'd lost my best friend. But Slate was an asshole and knew exactly what he wanted.

Cherry Popper

He wanted to fuck the next virgin…and then the next. Now he was bored with me. So why should I say no to the handsome man I admired? I didn't owe Slate anything—and he clearly didn't think he owed me anything. "Yeah…I think it is."

19

Slate

I TOLD MONROE WHAT WOULD HAPPEN.

It wasn't my fault she didn't believe me.

I didn't want a relationship, and despite my fondness for her, that wouldn't change. I paid her for a service, and once that service was fulfilled, I had no use for her. The transaction was complete—and so was our interaction.

Maybe that made me an asshole, but I had to make a clean break. I didn't want her to think there was hope that I would come back to her. I had to be firm, so firm that I wouldn't even take her calls. It would make this process easier for her.

I hadn't been with anyone else. I didn't rush to the next woman in line because I'd been busy with work and other things. And I found myself beating off to the memory of my night with Monroe, remembering every detail of her tight pussy. I'd never popped a better cherry, and I wanted to do it over and over again indefinitely.

Too bad that wasn't possible.

Whoever came next would be a disappointment compared to Monroe. But after I had enough lovers, I would slowly forget about her.

I was home when my mother spoke through the intercom. "Honey, I was in the neighborhood and wanted to see if I could stop by."

I pulled on a shirt then hit the button, allowing her to rise to my floor and step inside my living room. "Hello, Mother." I greeted her with a hug then immediately poured her a glass of wine. "What brings you by?"

She glanced around the apartment, like she was searching for someone besides me. "I was just in the neighborhood. Simone and I met for lunch to talk about the details for the wedding. The ceremony will be simple, but beautiful."

I tried not to think about that manipulative bitch, but I couldn't escape her. Soon, she would have my last name and a portion of my company. She would divorce Coen quickly and send our daily activities into a tailspin. "I warned Coen about her. He refuses to listen to me."

"There's nothing we can do. So just let it be."

"Nothing we can do?" I asked incredulously. "Your son is marrying a gold digger. That doesn't concern you?"

"It does concern me." She stood in skintight jeans, colored pumps, and a teal blouse. Her hair was short and styled, and she looked like a woman who belonged in fashion. "But if I nag at him, you know what's going to happen? He'll cut me it out of his life altogether. While I don't agree with this situation, there's nothing I can do about it. He's a grown man—and has to make his own mistakes."

My head was about to explode. "She's going to get her hands on our family money."

She sighed slightly. "I realize that. But again, there's nothing I can do. We should be grateful you and Coen own it equally, that way she can't take more than twenty-five percent. And perhaps Coen will see reason before it's too late."

I shook my head. "Not gonna happen. I told him she threatened me, and he didn't believe it."

"Threatened you how?"

"She admitted she was only after his money, and if I got in the way, she would make my life hell. I told Coen anyway, but he doesn't find me credible. He thinks this is all because I used to date her…even though that's the last thing on my mind."

She crossed her arms over her chest. "I'll try to talk to him one more time. There's not much time before the wedding."

Before he signed over his soul to the devil.

"Speaking of women…I heard you brought a date to the charity event." Mother watched me with her brown eyes, seeing what I would say in response.

"Yes…people bring dates to those sorts of things."

"Coen mentioned you were affectionate." She pressured me with her eyes, wanting me to spill my private life to her.

"Instead of paying attention to me, he should pay attention to his own date."

"I haven't heard of you taking a date to anything in five years," she said. "In fact, the media has never photographed you with anyone. Slate, are you gay? Because if you are, that's fine. No necessity in hiding it."

It was so ludicrous, I almost laughed. "No, Mother. I'm definitely not gay." I was obsessed with a very specific kind of pussy.

"Then is this woman special to you?"

"No. She's just a friend." A friend I would never speak to again. The thought made me sad.

"One that you kiss and touch?" she asked incredulously.

"A bit nosy, aren't we?" I countered.

"Well, I've never seen you with a woman besides Simone. I was excited to know you were on the mend."

"I never needed to mend." If she were anyone else, I would tell her to shut up and get out of my penthouse. "I'm just very picky. I don't have relationships in the public spotlight. I'm private about my personal life."

"So you do have women in your life?"

Not in the way she wanted. "Yes."

"But you liked this woman enough to make it public?"

"No."

"You never bring a date, so why did you bring one this time—"

"Enough." I held up my hand and silenced her, not feeling an ounce of guilt for shutting her down. She invaded my privacy when it was none of her business.

She seemed more concerned with who I was fucking instead of worrying about Coen's soon-to-be ex-wife. "If I'm ever ready to talk about someone, I'll talk about it. But right now, there's nothing to tell."

―――――

MAX PLACED the picture in front of me. "Her name is Trina. She's twenty-one."

I glanced at her picture, liked everything I saw, and then handed the picture back to him. "Yes."

"Alright." He returned the photo to his folder. "I'll make sure she's ready for Friday evening. Anything else?"

"No."

Max left my office.

I watched him go, feeling the weight of the guilt on my chest. A part of me knew I didn't want Trina at all, that I was just forcing myself into bed so I would forget about Monroe. If I called Monroe and told her I made a mistake, she would probably forgive me, but that wasn't what I wanted.

I had to move on.

Spending the month with Monroe had fucked with my head. It made me wonder if monogamy would be as bad as it was last time. It made me wonder if Monroe was someone I could actually trust. She was nothing like Simone, so that was the last thing I had to worry about.

But I didn't want to go down that road again.

To look like a fool in front of the whole world.

I was still paying the price for my mistake with

Simone. She was marrying my brother, while everyone looked on and thought it was the strangest family situation of all time. I looked like the idiot anyone could just walk all over, and my brother looked like the bigger idiot.

Simone tainted the Remington name.

Maybe if Simone had disappeared, I would have been able to forget about it. But since she was constantly around the corner, I could never get enough space to put this in the past. Her betrayal haunted me. My brother's betrayal haunted me even more.

AFTER I HIT the gym and showered, I sat on the couch and turned on the TV. The maid had the TV on while she cleaned, so the gossip channel was always the first thing to pop up when I hit the power button.

There was a story about Wyatt Newport, the CEO of the iconic fashion company, Silk. And of course, the media scrutinized his love life like private detectives. There was a short video of him having dinner with a woman in a nice restaurant.

But upon closer examination, I recognized the woman.

Monroe.

I turned up the volume. "Wyatt Newport is reported to be dating someone new after his very public breakup with model Sophia Lerange. He was spotted having an intimate dinner with a new interest at the French bistro on Lexington and 22nd street. They seemed to be having a good time. When our team asked for confirmation on this new romance, Wyatt Newport failed to reply."

I paused the screen so I could get a better look at the woman across from him. With that brown hair, beautiful neck, and the little freckles I loved to look at when she was underneath me, it was definitely her.

Monroe was dating someone else.

She didn't sit around and wait for me. She didn't cry every night while watching TV. She'd put her heart on the line, and when I stomped on it, she moved on. Now she was dating a man just as wealthy as I was—and handsome.

I was furious.

Fucking furious.

I gripped the remote so hard I popped the back compartment that contained the batteries. My teeth ground together with alarming pressure. If I pressed any harder, I might grind my teeth down to the root. It was the same rage I felt when I caught Simone with Coen—like I'd been betrayed.

Rage. Jealousy. Pain.

I felt it all.

I'd just picked out a new woman to fuck, but this still pissed me off.

She was seeing someone else, a man who had the looks and wealth to rival me.

I had no right to be angry, not after what I did to her. I shouldn't feel jealousy either, not when I said I wanted nothing to do with her. All these feelings were inappropriate. I should just change the channel and forget I saw it in the first place.

But I couldn't.

I couldn't stop staring.

―――――

NOW I GOOGLED WYATT CONSTANTLY, seeing if he'd spent any more time with Monroe. He owned a fashion company, so perhaps they were conducting a job interview in that restaurant. It would be unusual for the CEO to concern himself with such insignificant matters, especially over dinner. So that didn't seem likely.

A few days later, they were photographed in the park together. Bright and early on Saturday morning, they went for a jog. Both dressed in their workout clothes, they jogged down the path, somehow smiling even though they were in the midst of exercising.

Jogging in the park on a Saturday morning wasn't something new couples did. They usually had to go on a few dates first because they did something so…casual. Wyatt clearly didn't care about being photographed with her, and since he'd seen her more than once, that probably meant he liked her.

How could he not like her?

She was perfect.

She was smart, beautiful, and real. She didn't play games and wore her heart on her sleeve. She comforted me when I needed it most, and she was an amazing kisser. She gave head like she'd done it a thousand times.

Had she done the same to him?

Cherry Popper

Had she fucked him yet?

She probably still felt like a virgin because she was so tight.

I didn't want Wyatt to find out.

This was exactly what I'd wanted, so I shouldn't care that she was seeing someone else. What did I expect her to do? Be alone forever? I guess I didn't expect to know anything about her personal life at all…because I never expected her to date a high-profile guy. Now the news was in my face.

I should brush it off, but I couldn't.

As time passed, I became more obsessed.

Was he fucking her?

Was he falling for her?

Did she think about me anymore?

Did she hate me?

She did warn me that she wouldn't wait around. And she made good on her threat.

When I couldn't take it anymore, I decided to head to her office. I could call her, but I feared she might not answer. That rejection would sting, and talking to her about this over the phone seemed lame anyway.

I greeted her assistant, who smiled when she recognized me. "Hey, Kathy. I just wanted to drop by and see if Monroe was free for lunch."

"Well, she left for lunch about an hour ago. She should be back any minute."

She was on a budget, and she would normally bring her lunch to work, so if she ate out, that probably meant someone else was paying for it.

Someone named Wyatt.

"Thanks, Kathy." Just as I turned around, I came face-to-face with Monroe. Her hair was curled and pinned back, and she wore a halter dress with a bright blue cardigan. A gold necklace hung around her throat, and she looked like she was enjoying the last week of summer before it was officially gone.

Monroe stared at me with narrowed eyes, not the least bit happy to see me there. She was confused, uncomfortable, and a little angry.

And of course, Wyatt was with her.

Wyatt stood beside her, dressed in a navy blue suit with a black tie. He held himself like a powerful man, unflinching in my presence. It wasn't clear if he knew about my relationship with Monroe, but he was restrained.

Monroe kept staring at me, her eyes shifting back and forth as she recovered from the shock. "What do you want, Slate?" The bitterness was unmistakable. She was just as pissed at me as she was when she left my penthouse. The rage burned in her eyes, along with the lingering effects of the heartbreak. She wasn't afraid to be cold to me in front of both her assistant and the new man she was seeing, making me a public enemy.

I hadn't anticipated this moment, and it was one of the rare times when I wasn't sure what to do. I was caught off-balance, no longer in my element. I was chasing down an old lover, furious that she was with someone else. I hadn't felt this way in a long time. "I was hoping we could talk."

"About?" She kept up her hatred.

I glanced at her assistant and Wyatt. "Perhaps we

could do this in private."

"I just had lunch, so I need to get back to work." She turned to Wyatt. "Thank you for lunch."

"Of course." He leaned down and kissed her on the mouth.

Right in front of me.

And she kissed him back.

Right in front of me.

He let the kiss linger longer than necessary before he walked off. He didn't introduce himself or ask who I was—so he probably recognized me.

When she looked at me again, she was pissed. "I need to get to work, Slate. I'll see you around." She walked around me.

"Monroe." I followed her, moving down the hallway to her office.

She halted and turned around. "I mean it. I have a meeting in fifteen minutes."

"Then have dinner with me after work. We'll talk then." Seeing Wyatt kiss her only made me hate this even more, only made me more jealous. If she kissed him, then what else had she done? Wyatt got laid all the time. I doubted he would wait around if she didn't put out.

"What's there to talk about, Slate?" She crossed her arms over her chest.

"You'll find out at dinner."

"I already have plans. I'm meeting Wyatt's friends tonight. I would much rather do that than spend another moment talking to you." She walked into her office and shut the door in my face.

Fuck, maybe I was too late.

I DIDN'T SLEEP much that night.

I kept wondering if she'd slept over at his place.

Was she fucking him as I sat there on the couch?

Did she prefer him over me?

Did she really hate me?

The next morning, I went to her office again, this time earlier. There was no way she was having lunch with Wyatt two days in a row, so the odds played in my favor. I checked in with her assistant then moved to her office door.

Just like yesterday, Monroe didn't look happy to see me. "Have you ever heard of a phone?"

"Would you have answered if I called?"

"I'd probably do the exact same thing you did to me," she said coldly.

I deserved that—big-time. "Have lunch with me."

"I'll pass." She turned back to her computer and ignored me in the doorway.

"Then I'll just stand here."

"I'm pretty sure that's a fire hazard."

"Then maybe we should have this conversation at lunch—away from your coworkers."

She turned in her desk chair and gave me a cold look. "You aren't the boss of me anymore, Slate. You paid for a service and received that service. Now I'm just a regular person like everyone else—and I don't owe you anything."

She backhanded me without raising her wrist. "Sweetheart, please."

She rolled her eyes. "Don't ever call me that again."

That stung too. "I'm not going to go away."

"Security can take care of that."

"And I can take care of security. I'm not going to disappear, so you may as well cooperate."

She logged out of her computer and rose from her seat. "Fine." She grabbed her purse and walked out with me, moving fast in her heels so she could keep distance between us.

We left the building and headed to the deli we'd been before.

She made sure to pay for her own food before she sat down.

I didn't fight her on it. I sat across from her but ignored my sandwich, knowing I had an enormous task in front of me.

She unwrapped her sandwich and took a bite, unaffected by this conversation. She hadn't seemed surprised to see me show up at her office, both yesterday and today. She only seemed annoyed. "What is it, Slate?"

I'd worked so hard to get her attention for fifteen minutes, but now that I was there, I didn't know where to start. I didn't even know what I wanted. All I knew was I didn't like the idea of her and Wyatt together.

"Slate?" she pressed, losing her patience. "You've pestered me for my attention, and now you have it. So what do you want?"

I forgot how beautiful she was, especially when she was pissed. Her bright eyes burned like smoldering embers, and her full lips were tight with rage. I'd been alone for the last few weeks, and instead of fantasizing about old lovers or porn, I always pictured her. "I'm sorry I was such an asshole to you."

"It's fine," she said quickly. "I got over it."

"I'm sorry all the same."

She took another bite of her sandwich. "You warned me this would happen. It's my fault for not listening to you. I thought you were just wounded, and once that wound finally healed, you would let someone in. But I was wrong…you're just an asshole. And that's fine. If that's who you want to be, then be that person."

"It's not who I want to be…" I'd never tried to be anything in particular. I just wanted to cut out the bullshit. I just wanted sex without worrying about betrayal. I wanted a foolproof way to make sure I was never publicly humiliated again.

"Doesn't seem that way."

I wanted to ask about Wyatt, but I felt like I had no right. It was none of my business what she did in her personal life. When she asked if I'd been with someone else, I refused to give her an answer.

"If that's all you wanted, I would rather take my food to go."

"You hate me that much?" I asked, wounded. She couldn't even share a meal with me.

"No." She looked me in the eye, her rage dying away slightly. "That's how much you hurt me, Slate."

I felt like she punched me in the gut.

"I thought we had something more than sex. I thought we had a connection. I thought I meant something to you…you certainly meant something to me. But then you dumped me in the coldest way possible—you wouldn't even take my phone call. It was like the previous month never happened. Obviously, I meant nothing to you. No one would treat someone like that if that weren't true."

My voice emerged, quiet. "It's not true. You did mean something to me. You *do* mean something to me."

"Really?" she asked, still suspicious. "So you're telling me that your sudden reappearance has nothing to do with Wyatt? He's been all over the news since he started dating me. I know you don't care for gossip, but I'm sure you heard about it."

I wanted to lie, but I knew I couldn't. "Yeah…I did hear about it."

She shook her head slightly. "That's the only reason you're here, isn't it?" Disapproval was heavy in her voice, like she was borderline disgusted with me. "I told you I wouldn't wait around for you."

"Yeah…I can see that."

"You're jealous. And I'm sure I would be jealous too if I had to hear about all your new conquests…"

Conquests that hadn't been made. "You're the last woman I slept with."

"You expect me to believe that?"

"Would I lie?" She could call me an asshole all she wanted, but I was definitely no liar.

She didn't challenge me again.

"Have you slept with him?"

She rolled her eyes. "I'm not going to answer you."

That made my stomach tighten in painful knots.

"So, what do you want, Slate? To apologize for being an asshole? You've done that, so we can wrap this up and go our separate ways."

If I walked out of there, I would just be a memory to her. The second Wyatt spotted me, he only wanted her more. Now another powerful man wanted her, and it only made her more desirable. Letting her go was my biggest mistake. "That's not the only reason I'm here."

"Then what is it? I have to get back to work soon."

I had no idea what I wanted. I had no idea where this was going to go. All I knew was I didn't want her to be with Wyatt—or anyone else for that matter. "I can't explain how angry I was when I saw you with Wyatt. It was like…someone reached inside my chest and yanked out my heart. I was jealous…I was livid…I was a million things. I tried to forget about it, but then I found myself looking up Wyatt all the time, wondering if you two were still dating. It started to suffocate me…kill me." That was the most honest I'd been in a long time. I didn't even know how I felt until I started talking out loud. "I didn't expect you to be with someone so soon, especially someone so similar to me. I haven't been able to stop thinking about it ever since…" I stared into her eyes and hoped I would see some sympathy.

She gave it to me—but only a little bit. "If I saw you with someone else, it would bother me too."

"It doesn't bother me. It *kills* me." It was worse than what Simone did to me. I couldn't stop picturing them together.

"What does that mean, Slate?"

I didn't have an answer.

"Do you want to be with me?"

I didn't know what I wanted. I didn't want her to end up with someone else, not when it hurt me this much, but I didn't know how to be in a relationship. I didn't know how to trust someone enough to even try. "I don't know…"

She raised an eyebrow. "You don't know? So, you don't want to be with me, but you don't want me to be with Wyatt? You do realize that makes you the biggest asshole on the planet, right?"

"That's not what I said."

"Then explain it to me." She crossed her arms over her chest and cocked her head to the side.

I should have come here with a better plan. I shouldn't have acted off my emotions so radically. I didn't want her to be with Wyatt, but I had nothing to offer her in return. "You know relationships are hard for me."

"Yes, I'm aware."

"So you can't expect me to give that to you."

"Then what do you expect me to do?" she asked incredulously. "Put my life on hold while you figure out what you want? Not gonna happen, Slate. Wyatt is a nice guy, and we have a lot in common."

"But you still want me." She hadn't shown it because she'd been so angry this entire time, but she had to still feel something for me. If not, she wouldn't be so angry. That rage came from somewhere—pain.

"Doesn't matter. I'll move on."

I felt my heart tighten in agony. "Sweetheart—"

"I told you not to call me that. We aren't together

anymore...not sure if we ever were."

She'd only slept in my bed once, but she'd been the only woman in my life for the past six weeks.

"I don't think you really want me, Slate. I just think you can't stand the fact that you didn't ruin me. I bounced back and found someone else. I didn't cry over you and wait around. Now I'm seeing a man who's just as handsome, charming, and successful. You can't stand it."

"That's not true, Monroe."

"Then what is true?" she countered. "If you want me, then prove it. Give me something real. I'm not asking for forever, just something. Give me a relationship, monogamy, dates...normal stuff."

The second I did that, I would be back in the situation I was in before. I would be at the mercy of a woman. She could betray me the way Simone betrayed me—and I would be even more bitter. I didn't care about giving up the women I would fuck. I cared about giving up myself, trusting someone in a way I hadn't in five years.

When I didn't respond, her eyes narrowed in disapproval. "I'm not her, Slate. I would never betray you."

"You don't think she said the same thing to me?"

"But you know me. Give me more credit than that."

"I thought I knew my brother, someone I've known my entire life. We're of the same blood—and he had no problem stabbing me in the back."

Her anger disappeared altogether, and now she showed her deep sadness. "Don't let them have this much power over you, Slate. Don't let them destroy your future. Don't let them ruin you like this. They were assholes, but I can promise you, not everyone is an asshole."

I wanted to believe her, but I couldn't stand the idea of her having any power over me. My brother owned half the company, and he might drag it into ruin because of his stupidity. People couldn't be trusted.

"Slate."

I leaned over the table and held her gaze.

"I didn't like you at first. You were so cold and brutal. But then I got to know you…and I really liked the man underneath that hard exterior. I looked forward to seeing you every day, and the night we were together, I wasn't scared at all. I felt closer to you, wanted more of you. You became my friend, my lover, and the person I trusted most. I say all of this because…I still feel that way. I'm angry at you for the way you treated me, but if you wanted to be with me, really be with me, I would give it a try. But if you can't offer that…then I have no reason to stay."

I shouldn't have expected a different response. She might want me, but not enough to deny herself what she deserved. I wasn't happy with her decision, but I respected it.

"So, can you not offer that?"

I didn't want to give the answer that would end this for good. I would have to forget about her, try not to think about where she was sleeping at night. Sometimes I wondered if I could try to make a relationship work, if I could take it one step at a time, but I knew I would only waste her time. "No."

20

Monroe

When he rejected me a second time, it hurt just as much as the first time.

Slate wanted me, but not enough to trust me.

Simone and Coen really messed him up, made it impossible for him to trust anyone. I was harmless, but he viewed me as a criminal. All his walls were up, and he wouldn't even let me get close enough to scale them.

A part of me wanted to try anyway, to take it slow until he learned to trust me, but if he wasn't willing to compromise with me, why should I compromise with him? He could push me away at any time, and I would have to start all over.

And heal my broken heart.

Wyatt had never asked about Slate, even after the awkward run-in at the office. Our relationship was still casual. We hadn't even slept together. We went on dates, made out on the couch, and then I went home.

It seemed too soon to sleep with someone else.

Wyatt seemed to understand that, so he never pushed me. He might be seeing someone else while he saw me, so he was still getting action. But since we weren't exclusive, it didn't bother me. It also didn't bother me because I was still hung up on Slate.

I would be hung up on him for a while.

Wyatt and I met up for lunch a few days later. We split a pizza and had a few sodas. The nice thing about Wyatt was he didn't order a salad every time we went out to eat. He ate real food like a normal person—and still kept up his physique. I hadn't seen him shirtless yet, but I imagined Slate was a lot more ripped because he was religious about his food choices.

Wyatt finished his slice then wiped his greasy fingers on a napkin. "Can I ask you something?"

"Sure."

"Is Slate Remington the guy you slept with?"

I wasn't allowed to confide that information to someone else, but I felt awkward lying to him about who I slept with. I was torn in two, unsure what kind of answer I should give. "You know…I can't really talk about him."

"So that's a yes," he said before he took a drink from his soda. "So you have a type—powerful men."

"Ugh, not really. My relationship with him just unfolded. And I was sitting in a bar drinking when you came on to me."

"And you said yes."

"Regardless of how powerful you were, I would have said yes."

"Why?"

"Because you're gorgeous."

He grinned wide, like those words perfectly stroked his ego. "Good answer."

"It's the truth." I picked up my second slice and took a bite.

"So what did he want the other day?"

"Who?"

"Slate Remington."

"Oh…" I turned quiet, unsure what to say. "You know, I'd rather not talk about him." I'd already said it once, but perhaps I needed to say it again.

"I'm not trying to be nosy. I just want to know where you stand with him. Is there a possibility you might get back together? I'm sure Slate heard that we were seeing each other, and if he has any brains, he would do something to keep you. You're gorgeous too."

My cheeks filled with a blush. "Uh, thanks."

"So?" he pressed.

"He apologized to me and admitted he was jealous."

"As he should be." He rested his elbows on the table and leaned toward me.

"But he wasn't willing to give me what I wanted."

"Which is?"

"A relationship. I'm not looking for marriage or a conversation about kids. I have time to worry about that later. But I just wanted something…some kind of foundation. He has trust issues, so he turned me down."

"So let me get this straight. After dropping you, he chases after you to tell you he's jealous and unhappy. But he's still not willing to be with you?"

"In so many words…"

"That's a bit douchey."

I shouldn't defend Slate's honor, but I felt like I had to. "He just has trust issues. He's been backstabbed one too many times."

"Didn't that thing happen with Simone like five years ago?"

I guess the whole world really did know about it. "Yes."

"And shouldn't he be over it by now?"

I shrugged. "That's his business."

"Well, if he's not an idiot, he should let it go."

But he was an idiot. He wasn't willing to trust me enough even to try.

"Honestly, people cheat all the time. That's just how the world works. For a businessman like him, I would assume he'd have a thicker skin than that."

I still felt loyalty to Slate even if I shouldn't, and I didn't like listening to Wyatt tear him down, especially when he didn't even know him. "Let's talk about something else."

"Sorry, I didn't mean to make you uncomfortable. I just kinda like you and want to know how likely it is that Slate will get his head on straight. Because you're clearly still into him."

I didn't deny it. "I don't think he'll ever get his head on straight."

"Well, that's good news for me."

Cherry Popper

I WAS LYING IN BED, trying to fall asleep when my phone rang.

I looked at the screen and saw Slate's name.

I hadn't expected to see his name on my phone ever again.

I should ignore him the way he ignored me, but since I couldn't sleep anyway, I took the call. I let my silence announce my presence.

He did the same.

The silence ensued, and we didn't speak a word to each other.

I wasn't even sure why he called. But I also wasn't sure why I didn't hang up. If this was really over, we shouldn't be talking to one another. It would just make moving on more difficult. "Yes?"

"What are you doing?" he asked, his voice deep and quiet.

"It's eleven. What do you think I'm doing?"

"I imagine you're in bed, alone, wearing cute panties and a baggy t-shirt."

"You paint a realistic picture. What are you doing?"

"I'm in bed—nude."

"You always sleep in the nude?" I asked, missing that perfect body and that tanned skin.

"Only when I jerk off."

My breath caught in my throat when I heard the sexy confession. "Are you doing that now…?"

"Just finished. The used tissues are on my nightstand."

"That's quite a picture…"

"Does it turn you on?"

I would be lying if I said it didn't. "Did you think about me?"

"Yes."

"Then yes."

He sighed into the phone. "Sweetheart…I miss you."

I didn't berate him for the nickname, not this time. "I miss you too."

"Don't fuck him."

"I've got to fuck someone sometime. I can't have great sex one time and then go celibate."

"So you liked it?"

"Obviously. I came twice, didn't I?"

"But you also cried most of the time."

Because I had an enormous dick in between my legs. "It was my first time…cut me some slack."

"I'm not judging you. It was sexy. Your cherry was my favorite to pop."

"Then why do you want to keep doing it with other people?"

He turned quiet. "It's not that I want to keep doing it…"

"You're stupid if you throw us away over something some bitch did to you five years ago. You know that, right? Because Wyatt really likes me…and I'm starting to really like him." Eventually, I would let myself really fall for him. Then Slate would become a distant memory.

He sighed into the phone. "Like I said, it's not about her. It's just… I don't see a lot of good in the world."

"You don't think I'm good?"

"I never said you weren't. But I really don't know you that well. We've only known each other for two months—and I haven't seen you much in the last few weeks."

"Then get to know me, Slate. I'm not asking for marriage or your pin number."

He chuckled. "I know."

"I'm not asking for anything…just for you to try."

"Even that is difficult for me. I've already let you in so much."

"Then keep going."

"Easier said than done."

I couldn't keep talking him into this. I couldn't entertain these late-night phone calls. "Slate, if that's your final decision, you have to stop calling me. I'm not yours to call. I'm going to keep seeing Wyatt…and soon, I'm going to start sleeping with him. Once that happens, I can't keep up this weird relationship with you. It would be deceitful."

He moaned into the phone like he was in pain. "I don't want to picture you with him…"

"Then don't. But it'll be a reality."

"That's even worse."

"Well, that's something you'll have to live with."

He turned quiet, his somber mood heavy over the line. "I'll let you go to sleep, sweetheart. Good night."

Just like the last time he rejected me, it hurt like hell. I didn't even bother saying goodnight before I hung up.

21

Slate

I SAT AT MY DESK AND STARED OUT THE WINDOW TO the city beyond.

My brother was getting married next week—and I'd never been more confused.

Monroe was out there, dating billionaire Wyatt Newton. He was just as rich as me, just as handsome, and he understood just how special she was. In a short amount of time, he would win over her affection—and fuck her.

That would kill me.

I wasn't just obsessed with Monroe because of her incredible pussy. I loved everything about her, from the freckles on her cheeks, to her full lips, to the way she laughed. I loved the way she licked her wine away when a drop came loose. I loved the way she pardoned me for my sins and saw me as a good man underneath. I also loved her purity—the fact that only I had fucked her.

The second someone else had her, I would lose a piece of her.

I didn't want that to happen.

But I couldn't give her what she asked.

So how did I accomplish both? How did I get her under my thumb without making a commitment I couldn't keep?

I stared out the window for twenty minutes until it came to me.

The perfect idea.

I SHOWED up at her apartment after work, hoping that asshole wouldn't already be there. I knocked on the door and waited. Once I heard the sound of her footsteps, I held my breath and waited. She would see my face in the peephole, and she would probably be annoyed I wasn't staying away from her.

She opened the door, wearing dark jeans and a white blouse that tied in front of her waist. She had red lipstick painted across her lips, thick mascara, and sexy eye shadow. She didn't wear a lot of makeup, but when she did, she was even more stunning. "Slate, what did we just—"

"I need to talk to you. Can I come in?"

She hesitated before she opened the door.

I stepped inside her cramped living room and finally felt some privacy once the door was shut.

She crossed her arms and looked at me, already disappointed by what I would say.

"I want to offer you something. It's the best compromise I can come up with."

"A compromise?" she asked. "I'm listening."

"You still have a $450,000 loan hanging over your head. Not only will you be paying that for the rest of your life, but you're going to have $2,000 plucked out of your bank account every month."

"Thank you for reminding me…"

"I'll pay it off for you—in exchange for something."

Her eyebrow cocked, and she looked offended rather than pleased.

"You. I want you for three months. And I'll wipe out your debt."

"You do realize that officially makes me a prostitute."

"I don't see it that way." I saw it as a way to keep her for a little longer, to get her out of my system so letting her go would be easier. "In addition, that also gives me time to try to be what you want. A test run."

She didn't reject it right away, but she didn't seem happy either. "So you're going to pay me for sex?"

"Not just sex. But you."

"Same thing."

"And I said I'm willing to try to be something more. We'll be monogamous. We'll do the dates and the relationship…and if I can't see it happening in three months…that'll be the end."

"And my heart will be broken into a million pieces."

So would mine. "That's the best offer I can give you. You're risking your heart, but at least you'll be out of debt for good."

"Slate, I want you for you. Not for your money."

"I know…but at least this gives you an incentive to give me a chance." If I'd asked without offering the money, she would never agree. She wouldn't risk getting her heart broken after three months with me. It was too risky, especially when I would probably leave anyway. But now she was cleaning up her debt for good. She would get a clean slate, a better chance of a quality life. She wouldn't have to work just to pay bills. She could save her money, get a better apartment, and maybe even buy a car.

She paced slowly as she shook her head. "You really don't want me to be with Wyatt, huh?"

"No." I couldn't stand the thought.

"It makes me sad to think he's the only reason this is happening. If I dated some nobody, you never would have known about it and never would have thought of me again."

Maybe I wouldn't have gotten jealous and marched to her office to get her back, but I certainly would have thought of her. "That's not true. If that were the case, I would have slept with someone before I even found out about Wyatt. But I haven't."

She stopped pacing and looked at me.

"Are you saying yes?"

"I don't know…"

I needed her to say yes. I needed to have her back. I needed to take her back to my penthouse so I could enjoy her, to have the real thing instead of a stale memory. "Say yes."

"I'm not sure if the money is worth a broken heart."

"But you might not have a broken heart. Maybe you'll get sick of me. Maybe you'll be the one who wants to leave."

She scoffed. "I highly doubt that, Slate."

"There's still a chance it could end differently."

"How good of a chance?" she whispered.

I wished I could be different. I wished I could be a normal man and give this woman what she wanted. Before Simone, I fooled around because I hadn't met a woman I actually liked. Then we got together, and monogamy was easy. But she took my virginity when we were young and then stabbed me in the back a decade later. I hadn't been the same since. I turned off my heart completely and turned into a fucking machine. But everything had been different with Monroe, since the moment she stormed into my office. "I don't know. But good enough to try."

22

Monroe

I didn't feel comfortable running off to Slate's penthouse right away, so I asked him to leave so I could break it off with Wyatt first. We weren't serious, but he had the right to know what was going on.

He took it well. Told me to call him if it didn't work out.

I suspected I would be making that phone call in a few months.

I sat in my office and considered the offer I'd agreed to. Three months for $450,000—that was over $100,000 every month. I was being paid to put my life on hold, to risk heartache for a man who couldn't commit. But I needed that money…and I needed him.

Maybe it was just an excuse to do something reckless. Most people wouldn't walk away from that kind of money, so it was a good reason to stay, a good reason to do something stupid. I wanted to believe there was a chance Slate might change, but in my heart, I found that unlikely.

But I wanted him anyway.

The second he got what he wanted before, he was so cold to me. I would never forget the dread in my stomach when he ignored my phone call, the way he looked so annoyed when I stopped by his penthouse.

He was a whole different person.

Once he popped my cherry, he turned back into the asshole I'd originally met.

Would he do it again?

I finished a day at the office, and just as I was walking out of the building, I ran into Slate.

In his suit and tie, he looked like a million dollars with his muscular physique. Ignorant to all the stares directed his way, he focused on me. He stopped in front of me on the sidewalk, one hand sliding into his pocket. He didn't greet me with affection like he would behind closed doors.

"What brings you here?" Now that he'd popped up at my apartment and my office, I was used to him catching me off guard.

"Haven't heard from you in a while."

"Just busy."

He'd just shaved that morning, so he looked particularly handsome. His brown eyes looked like melted chocolate that was perfect for dipping. His dark hair was nearly the same color as his eyes, so he had a naturally intense appearance. Even when he was at his sweetest, he was still threatening. "Have you thought about my offer?"

This would probably be a mistake, but maybe it wouldn't be a mistake I would regret. "I ended things with Wyatt yesterday. He took it well."

Relief danced across his eyes like it was the best news he'd heard all day. His shoulders relaxed noticeably with the deep breath he took. His rival was out of the way, which meant he had me all to himself. "I'm surprised he was so understanding."

"He told me to call him if it doesn't work out."

The relief he showed a second ago disappeared. "Of course he did…"

"If you don't want me, someone else will. It's not that surprising."

"It's not surprising at all…just annoying."

I stepped around him and headed to the sidewalk. "You could have called."

"I don't like talking on the phone."

"But you like sitting in traffic for fifteen minutes?"

His hand moved to the small of my back as he stopped me on the sidewalk. "Come over." He nodded to his car sitting at the curb.

"You don't waste any time, do you?"

He brought me in close, his face just inches from mine. "When I said I missed you, I meant it."

After the terrible way he'd treated me, I wasn't eager to get back into bed right away. He took my virginity then pretended I didn't exist. The last time I was in that penthouse, he treated me like I was nothing but a nuisance, a stranger. "I'm not ready to pick up where we left off. Just because I agreed to this doesn't mean I'm not mad at you. It doesn't mean I'm ready to open my legs and fuck you."

If he was disappointed, he pretended otherwise. "Then let's have dinner. I'll cook for you."

"Will you make salad?"

The corner of his mouth rose in a smile. "Maybe as an appetizer."

"Alright. I'll be there in a few hours." I stepped away from his grasp so I could walk up the sidewalk.

He pulled me close then placed a kiss on my mouth, kissing me for the entire world to see. His hands guided me farther into his chest, and he slowly caressed my lips, making love to them in a way he never made love to my pussy. He breathed into me gently before he pulled back. His hands loosened on my body before he turned away. "I'll see you soon."

IT WAS the last week of summer, so I wore my sundresses as much as possible. Summer was my favorite season because getting ready for work was super easy. I just pulled on a dress with a cardigan or jacket, added some accessories, and then I walked out the door. Once it became winter, I would have to pull on my skintight jeans, boots, layers upon layers of warmth, until I was left feeling suffocated in the bulky clothing.

I changed into a navy blue dress with strappy sandals before I headed to his penthouse on the other side of town. It was a train ride away and then a few blocks of walking, but since I sat at a desk all day long, I didn't mind it.

I took the elevator to his floor then stepped inside to the smell of dinner in the kitchen. "Something smells good." I set my purse on the entryway table and relived the memory of the last time I was there. He sat on the couch with a drink in his hand, shirtless and hostile.

"Chicken Picatta. And you're right on time." He got up to set the plates on the dining table then walked to me, wearing just his sweatpants low on his waist. His upper body was muscular and strong, chiseled with powerful muscles and sexy golden skin. He greeted me by the door by moving his hand into my hair and kissing me passionately on the lips. His arm circled my waist, and he pulled me close as he treasured me, apologizing for the harsh way he'd treated me the last time I was there with his lips but not his words.

Every time he kissed me, my anger died away a little more. Wyatt was a good kisser, also handsome and charming, but I didn't feel the same sparks with him that I did with Slate. There was a special affection for Slate inside my heart, a place only he had claimed. If I ever wanted to feel something real for someone else, I would have to erase him from my heart completely.

But that seemed impossible.

He pulled away and looked at me with possession, a new look I hadn't received before. Now that I was in his arms once again, he didn't want to let me go.

Maybe he would appreciate me this time. Maybe he wouldn't let me go because he didn't want anyone else to have me. It wasn't romantic, but it was better than nothing.

His hand slackened against my hair, and he stepped away. "Hope you're hungry."

"My diet consists of mostly peanut butter and jelly sandwiches, so yes, I'm hungry."

"Those are good—once in a while."

"Wait…you've had one?" I followed him to the dining table. "I thought you didn't eat carbs."

"Not usually. But I've had a few sandwiches here and there." He poured two glasses of wine and sat across from me, our hot meals emitting steam because they were so warm. Grilled chicken with lemons and capers along with a side of broccoli. It was still a boring dinner, but delicious all the same.

I cut into my dinner and started to eat. "You're a pretty good cook. I've never had the time or the money."

"You will soon enough. Maybe you could take it up then."

I couldn't imagine life without that debt hanging over my head. I was still getting used to having some extra cash because my student loans had been wiped out. What would it be like not to have all that money drained out of my account every month? My medical bill was more expensive than my rent.

There was a check sitting on the table, so he placed it in front of me. "I would rather you used it now. It would save you a bit of cash."

I always felt uncomfortable taking his money. Up

until that point, I never had. I pushed the check back. "When service is complete, we'll talk about it."

"Or you could take it now…and be obligated to complete the service."

"You think I'm going anywhere?" I asked incredulously. "The money is just my way of justifying my decision…but I care about it the least."

He didn't push the check back at me again. He let it sit on the table, forgotten.

I kept eating, trying to pretend that interaction didn't happen. I felt like Julia Roberts in *Pretty Woman*. This whole thing started because I needed money, but now I needed him more. I felt like a prostitute who only wanted one client.

Slate kept eating, his eyes watching my face most of the time. He always ate with his body hunched over his food, his muscular arms rippling with the movements. The veins along his skin were prominent, thick cords that were defined just underneath his tanned flesh. He was hairless with the exception of his face, where his beard constantly regrew. By tomorrow morning, he would have a significant shadow across his face. "My brother is getting married on Saturday."

"Unless he's marrying a new woman, I guess that means he still won't listen to you."

He shook his head. "I told my mother to talk to him, but she said it was a lost cause. If she pushes him anymore, she's afraid she'll lose him altogether."

"Maybe that's what he needs to learn his lesson."

"He's going to learn his lesson…but it's going to be in

the most brutal way possible." He ate much quicker than I did, devouring his food in a few bites. His eyes held his resentment for both Simone and Coen, the two people he despised most on this planet. "When that moment comes, I won't laugh in his face…but I'll say I told you so."

"It'll probably be unnecessary at that point. Have you tried recording her? Getting evidence?"

"I wired my office with mics just in case, but she hasn't made any moves. She's not stupid. Now that I officially know what she's doing, she'll play it safe until that marriage license is signed—without a prenup."

"I guess that makes sense. So there's nothing you can do."

He shook his head. "It's his funeral."

"Are you going to the wedding?"

He nodded. "I have to."

"You don't have to do anything. No one would judge you for not going."

"But my mother wants me to be there. Now that my father is gone, I know she feels alone. At least if I'm there, she won't feel so lonely. I look a lot like my father, so sometimes when she looks at me, it makes her feel better, like he's still here."

"Well…he's always here. As long as you think about him, he always will be." That's how I felt about my mother. She crossed my mind often, when there was something interesting going on in my life that I would normally tell her, I wondered what her response would be. I visited her grave on the anniversary of her death and her birthday every year.

"True."

"It's a small wedding?"

"Just some friends and family."

I wondered if he would take me along, but when he didn't say anything, I assumed that wasn't the case. Perhaps it was too public for him. I assumed he would want some comfort during the difficult time, a distraction from the living nightmare.

I finished my food until there was nothing left. "That was delicious. Where do you get your recipes?"

"Online. Sometimes my mom gives me a few of hers. This is one of them."

"Pretty good."

"And easy. I don't like anything that takes more than thirty minutes."

I never spent any time in the kitchen, unless I was pressing two slices of bread together and making a sandwich. When I went to the grocery store, I only picked up the essentials, like milk and cereal along with my shampoo and conditioner. "Maybe you can teach me sometime."

"Sure. But I have one condition."

"Alright."

"You have to be naked."

"I'm not going to cook naked," I said with a laugh. "Oil will splash all over me, and that will hurt."

"Fine. Lingerie."

"That's not any better."

"One or the other—it doesn't matter to me."

"You're such a perv." I picked up both plates and carried them to the sink in the kitchen. I rinsed them off so his maid wouldn't have so much work to do in the morning. When I came back to the table, Slate had finished his wine, but the nearly full bottle remained on the table.

He watched me sit across from him. "I am a perv—and I won't bother denying it."

"At least you admit your faults."

"I wouldn't describe it as a fault, but a quality. I enjoy sex more than most men. I've always been that way, even before I was the Cherry Popper."

"By the way, I told Wyatt I sold my virginity for money. This was before I knew who he was. When you showed up at my office during lunchtime and he saw you...he put the pieces together. I know I signed that NDA and I didn't give him your name, but I didn't mean to betray your trust. It just happened."

Slate didn't seem angry. "Why did you tell him that in the first place?"

"Because I went straight to a bar after I left your place. I'd been drinking, and he joined me...and I told him why I was hitting the liquor so hard." I had no idea he was Wyatt Newton, and I had no idea he would run into Slate.

He shrugged. "All powerful men have dirty secrets. Wyatt is no different."

"He seemed nice to me."

"Trust me, he's not. All men are pigs, but the rich can afford their fantasies."

"I don't know if I believe all men are pigs...but I think most are."

"More than most." He finished the last of his wine then leaned farther over the table so he could get a better look at me. "You know what my life has been like the last couple of weeks?"

I waited for his answer.

"All I did was work, workout, and then jerk off. My life was the same routine every single day. It wouldn't have been so bad if I weren't so depressed. I'd be in the middle of a meeting, and an image of you two would pop up in my head… It haunted me. I kept wanting to get you back, but I didn't have anything to offer you. I told myself I was doing the right thing, that I wouldn't change for you. But every time Max found me a woman, I turned him down. Instead of popping cherries like before, I was just alone. That's what my life has been like…"

"Sounds lonely."

"It was. I used to love being alone, but then it felt empty."

If he felt that way, how could he let me go in the first place? "You were such an asshole to me. It was like you were a different person."

"I know…" He bowed his head in shame.

"Why were you like that?"

"I needed to convince you that I was serious."

"You could have done that in a much nicer way."

"Maybe," he said. "But I don't know how to be nice."

"You're being nice right now."

"I can't control when it happens."

"I think you can." I grabbed the bottle and refilled both of our glasses. Now that dinner was finished and we were alone together, staring into each other's eyes with longing, it seemed like sex was on both of our minds. Ever since the first time I'd had it, I'd been thinking about it, wanting to come like that again. I wondered if it would hurt like last time. I wondered if he would have to stretch me out a couple of times before the pain stopped altogether.

Slate stared at me like he was thinking the same thing, but he refused to act on it. I told him I didn't want to sleep with him right away, and he seemed to take that request seriously. "If you took my check and paid off the loan, would you consider moving closer into the center of Manhattan?"

"No," I said with a laugh. "All the money I spent on loans would just go to rent. I'll never be able to afford anything by Central Park. I can barely afford the subway."

"Do you intend to live in the city forever?"

"I always assumed I would get married, so we would be able to afford a townhouse much closer. Assuming he has a decent job and we can split the mortgage." I wouldn't be able to manage anything on my own, unless I was promoted to a much higher position.

"Or you could marry a rich guy." Slate said the words as he looked me in the eye. "Then you could afford to live anywhere you want."

I didn't know if he was referring to himself or to Wyatt. "We'll see what happens. I'm young, and I have some time before I start worrying about it."

"You aren't in a hurry to settle down?"

"No. If it's meant to happen, it'll happen, whether I'm thirty or forty."

"You have a long way before you turn thirty."

I shrugged. "No good comes from expectations. If you set expectations for yourself and don't meet them, you're just setting yourself up for sadness, especially when it's arbitrary. I'm not in a hurry to be anywhere at any specific time. Where life takes me…it'll work out."

He smiled. "That's a good philosophy."

"I think so too." I took a long drink of my wine then left the empty glass on the table. If I kept drinking like this, I wouldn't be able to find my way home. Now his bed seemed more appealing, especially when his sweaty body was on top of mine. "I should go. Thank you for dinner."

"Of course." He rose from the chair and walked me to the door. There was no argument about getting me to stay. There was one thing he wanted from me above all else, but he didn't pressure me. "My driver will take you home."

"He doesn't need to do that."

"He's on the clock—may as well give him something to do." He hit the button on the elevator so the doors opened. "Have dinner with me tomorrow."

"Sure."

He circled his arms around me and brought me close into his chest. He restrained his kiss and pressed his forehead against mine as he held me on the threshold. His large hands spanned across my back completely, and he slowly moved them up as he brought me in even closer. When one of his hands reached my hair, he fisted it and gave me a deep kiss.

The kiss was just as good as the one he greeted me

with. Full of passion, heat, and adoration. He cradled my head and kept me close to him, letting me feel his breath fill my lungs. His other hand snaked down to my ass, and he pulled my dress up so he could squeeze my bare cheek. He moaned as he kissed me, like he missed my ass as much as the rest of me.

If this kept going, I would be naked in no time.

I pulled away and licked my lips. "Good night."

His hands didn't release me right away, like he had to fight himself to be a gentleman. He lowered his hands away from my ass and hit the button again since the doors had shut. "Good night, sweetheart. I can call you that again, right?"

I stepped inside the elevator so he wouldn't try to kiss me again. "Yes." I held his gaze as I watched the door close, knowing he was hard in his sweatpants because I'd felt it right against me. I knew his fingers would be wrapped around his length tonight, thinking of me, just as I would be thinking about him with my fingers under my panties.

I SAT across from Slate at the table in the restaurant. The wine bottle sat on the surface, and both of our glasses were full. Our entrees had been selected, and now we sat there in silence because there wasn't much to say.

We were running out of things to talk about.

The basis of our relationship was sex, so it was impossible to think about anything else. Slate wanted it from me and I wanted it from him, but would it happen? I didn't know. But when he stared at me like that across the table, I felt like the prey he would dominate the second we were alone together. This dinner seemed like a pointless task.

"Sweetheart?"

I drank my wine before I set the glass down. "Yes?"

"Do you know how to touch yourself?"

The question caught me off guard, especially since the tables around us were filled with other people. Conversations were loud, dishes clanked against tables, and utensils chattered, so our quiet words probably faded away, but it was still a question that should only happen behind closed doors. "Why do you ask?"

He wore a dark blue t-shirt with denim jeans, refusing to adhere to the dress code of nicer restaurants. He still wore his Omega watch on his wrist, so that hinted at the wealth sitting in his back pocket. His face was always his ticket inside any place, because most people in the money world knew exactly who he was. "You're inexperienced. I'm just curious to know how inexperienced you are."

"That would mean I haven't had an orgasm in twenty-three years."

He shrugged. "You haven't had sex in twenty-three years. That's even more shocking."

"Yes…I know how to touch myself." Heat moved up my neck and into my cheeks. It was an embarrassing question, and I had an embarrassing answer.

Slate's reaction didn't indicate his feelings on the matter. He stared at me without blinking, several heartbeats passing. His dark eyes hinted at the darkness in his soul, his disturbing tastes. "Did you do it last night?"

"That's a personal question…" When we shared that kiss by the elevator, my back wanted to hit his mattress and my thighs wanted to separate. All my logic disappeared when his mouth was on mine, sucking my soul right from my lips. I left his penthouse unsatisfied, and even after the fifteen-minute drive home, I was still charged.

"The second you were gone, I stripped out of all my clothes, got into bed, and pulled out an enormous bottle of lube from my nightstand." He described his solo event with little regard for the people around us. It didn't seem like he cared if he was overheard or not. He painted a vivid picture of his evening with his hand. "I dumped it all over my length, closed my eyes, and pictured that night we had together. The tears in your eyes…the way your tits bounced…the way you clawed at me when you both enjoyed it and felt the pain. I squeezed my hand as hard as I could to replicate the feeling of your unbelievably tight pussy, but I couldn't. I've fucked a lot of cunts in the last five years, and none of them compare to yours. I only lasted a few minutes before I exploded onto my chest, pretending I was stuffing your pussy with come."

I was mesmerized by the imagery, imagining his sexy, naked physique on the bed with his hand wrapped around his impressive length. My mouth suddenly felt dry, so I took a drink of my wine to make it moist again. The restaurant had felt cool a moment ago, but now I felt like I was in the desert on a hot summer day.

Slate watched me battle my discomfort. "What about you?"

"What makes you think I did the same?"

"That kiss in front of the elevator. I thought it would be enough to make you stay."

It nearly had.

"So?" he pressed. "I shared my story. Now share yours."

I was equally aroused and humiliated by the conversation. It was too intimate for a public place, but the discussion happened anyway. Hopefully, the waitress didn't walk over at the wrong moment. "Yes."

"Yes, what?"

"I did."

He tilted his head slightly. "Give me more than that, sweetheart. I rushed to the bedroom without even putting the bottle of wine away. The glasses were left there until morning, when the maid cleaned them up. I had to jerk off so bad that nothing else mattered. And that's all you're going to give me?"

"Alright…I came home, left my shoes by the door, and then changed into my baggy t-shirt before I got into bed. I brought my knees to my chest and opened myself wide before I rubbed my finger against my clit."

His eyes narrowed as he listened to me, probably imagining my story the way I imagined his.

"My eyes were closed…and I thought about our first time together. I thought about your expression, the way your jaw was clenched so tight, like you couldn't enjoy it too much without exploding. I thought of the way it hurt…the way it felt good."

Slate hung on every word, his jaw slowly tightening and his eyes burning.

I thought he might lunge at me over the table.

"Are you happy?" I asked, grabbing my glass again.

He didn't blink as he stared me down, his expression still focused with laser precision. "Yes. Very."

AFTER WE FINISHED DINNER, we got into the back seat of his car.

"My place or yours?" He asked the same question every single time we got into the town car.

But I was surprised he'd asked it at all. After the conversation we'd had, it seemed like we both wanted the same thing.

He stared straight ahead. "Think about it. The second we're inside my penthouse, I'm ripping off your clothes and taking you to bed. Nothing will stop me. So if you aren't ready, tell me to take you to your place. That's the only place where you'll be safe." He placed his arm on the armrest as he looked out the window, the darkness illuminated by the street lights and business signs. The middle divider was up, so he spoke without fear of being overheard. He probably would have said the exact same thing anyway even if his driver could hear. "What's it gonna be?"

I had no intention of going home alone and touching myself. I was still disappointed in Slate for the way he treated me, but I couldn't resist him anymore. It'd been nearly a month since the last time we were together. My anger couldn't keep me away from him much longer. "Your place."

"Thank fucking god." He hit the button so he could speak through the intercom. "My place, Tim." He lowered his hand and looked at me, his muscular chest stretching the front of his t-shirt, making it tight against his physique. His hand moved to my thigh, his fingers touching my bare skin because my dress had risen when I sat down. He gave me a gentle squeeze. "Is your shot still current?"

"Yes." It hadn't been three months yet, but I didn't want to start then stop, so I'd already made an appointment for the next one. My insurance covered it anyway. Besides, I thought I would have a regular sex life whether Slate and I worked out or not.

"Good." Instead of looking out the window like he usually did, he stared at me, watching me with those dark eyes that matched the nighttime around us. His fingers caressed me, lightly rubbed my soft skin. "How do you want it, sweetheart?"

I gave him a blank look. "What do you mean?"

"You're still new to this. How do you want me to take you?"

"I didn't think I had much of a choice in the matter."

"You always have choices—with me."

Just because my virginity was gone didn't mean I wanted to fuck hard like I was broken in. I wanted to take it slow, for him to be gentle. "Like last time, but easy…"

Slate didn't seem disappointed. "Easy it is."

SLATE MADE good on his threat.

Once we were inside his penthouse, he was on me fast. His hand snaked into my hair, and he pressed me against the wall as he kissed me. Aggressive and territorial, he smothered me with his rock-hard body and stole the air directly out of my lungs. With a single hand, he popped the button of his jeans and pulled down the zipper so his pants would start to sag. He hiked my leg over his hip and ground his fat cock against my panties as he kissed me, so hard that his erection must have started back in the car.

My dress was bunched up at my waist, and I felt my panties grow wet as he continued to grind against me, pressing my clit like a magic button. My hands gripped his shoulders, and I felt my body smash into the wall, my mouth suffocated by his kisses. I started to grind back against him, my panties growing so wet they stained his boxers.

He kept one hand anchored in my hair as he kissed me, like there was any possibility I would get away from him. His intensity didn't fluctuate as he kissed me, his passion burning bright in his kiss and his thrusts.

A man had never kissed me like this before, had never made me feel overpowered. I was up against the wall with a wet thong, growing impatient because I wanted that cock inside me, not just against my clit.

He must have grown impatient too, because he scooped up my other leg and lifted me against his chest. He kicked away his jeans and carried me across the living room and into the hallway, his face pressed close to mine with heated breaths. He didn't kiss me, but he stared at me instead, and that seemed to make it more intimate, with just the connection of our eyes.

He laid me on the bed before he pulled his shirt over his head, revealing the perfect body I'd pictured in my mind last night. He gripped the strap of my thong and slowly pulled it down, getting it off my legs and to my ankles. My dress was still on, but he didn't bother taking it off.

I pulled his boxers over his ass so his cock could be free. I pushed them down to his thighs and let them sit there, knowing they would come off on their own.

He slipped two fingers inside me without warning, getting past my entrance easily. When he closed his eyes and moaned, it was obvious he'd found what he was looking for. "Sweetheart, you're so wet." He removed his fingers then sucked them. "Ready for me." He opened the drawer to his nightstand and grabbed the bottle of lube he smeared on his length when he jerked off.

Just looking at the bottle turned me on.

He spread the lubricant all over his length, rubbing it on his balls too. He closed the bottle and left it on the bed as he separated my thighs, hooking his arms behind my knees. He held his heavy body on top of mine then pressed his thick crown to my entrance. "You look even more beautiful than last time." He slowly sank inside me, pressing his thick head past my small lips. "And just as tight." He paused as he closed his eyes and enjoyed it.

"Maybe you just have a big dick…" I breathed as he

stretched me, panted as he tried to fit the enormous cock in my small channel.

He opened his eyes and sank a little deeper. "I do have a big dick, sweetheart. But you have virgin pussy—very virgin pussy." His rock-hard cock slowly moved past my tightness, taking advantage of our mutual slickness to get inside. He got a little deeper every few seconds, slowly sliding into me until he fit most of his length.

It hurt like last time. It didn't matter how open my legs were. It didn't matter that it wasn't my first time. His big dick was still too large for me, and fucking me once wasn't enough to stretch me out. It felt like a thick metal pipe had been shoved between my legs—hard as steel.

Slate watched my reaction to him, watched the way I struggled to take him. "I'm popping your cherry all over again."

"It feels that way…"

He hadn't even started to thrust yet. He held himself on top of me as he gave my body a chance to get used to him, to stretch so it wouldn't be so painful. His arms kept my thighs apart so he could easily fit his big length inside me. His heavy breaths filled the space around us, his arousal audible in every breath he took. The longer he stared at me, the more his length thickened. It even twitched, even though there wasn't much room for it to move. "It's gonna take the full three months just to break you in." He started to thrust, to gently move his dick in and out of me.

I rocked with his thrusts, feeling his enormous dick move in and out as my body shook with the movements.

Cherry Popper

His gargantuan size almost seemed too big, too unnatural. He wasn't the kind of man who should be a woman's first lover. Maybe I should have started on a smaller scale, a man with a normal-sized dick.

As much as I tried to resist, the tears formed in my eyes. It was such a visceral kind of pain, and in a twisted way, I enjoyed the way it hurt. I enjoyed the fact that he was such a big man that my pussy could barely take him.

He pressed his forehead to mine and moaned as he continued to thrust, turned on by the sight of my tears. "You're pretty when you cry." His long cock slid in and out, nearly tapping against my cervix every single time. He watched the tears streak down my cheeks as he gave me his cock over and over. He started to moan repeatedly, as if the scene in front of him was too erotic to handle. "Fuck, you make me wanna come, sweetheart."

"You better not. Not until I'm finished."

He stopped his thrusts when he was deep inside me, the look in his eyes smoldering. He leaned his head down and kissed me slowly on the mouth, our lips barely moving together. His cock was still pulsing inside me, eager to keep going. Then he started to move again, this time dragging his body right over my clit.

Now the pain was insignificant.

He rocked into me nice and slow, moving into me at a much slower pace than the last time we were together. He continued to kiss me, his lips loving and soft. His moans stopped altogether because he was focused on me, focused on pushing me past the finish line so he could find his release.

It didn't take long. The tears stopped falling, and my lips trembled against his. I could feel the explosion in the distance, the fast-approaching hurricane that was about to break the storm. My legs widened, and my pussy tightened in preparation for the all-consuming pleasure I was about to feel. My toes curled prematurely, and I started to whisper his name before the climax even hit. "Slate…" I gripped his ass with both hands and guided him into me, wanting him to rub my clit at the perfect spot. I wanted his cock deep inside me even if it still hurt. I wanted all of him, to feel every single inch before I fell over the edge. "God…" The orgasm went nuclear, detonating all my nerves and muscles as the pleasure made its way throughout my entire body. The climaxes I had alone in my bedroom were nothing compared to the ones he gave me. This felt like the end of the world but also the beginning. I screamed against his face as my nails dug deep into his tight ass. "Slate…" If sex was always this good, I shouldn't have waited so long. It was a spiritual experience, the closest touch to heaven I would ever receive until my time on earth was over. It was indescribable, having a man deep inside me as I came around him.

His thrusts slowly increased because he couldn't contain himself any longer. It'd been weeks with no sex, so it wasn't surprising he couldn't last. He'd been jerking off with his hand and some lube, but that wasn't the same as the real thing…as I quickly learned. He looked into my eyes as he gave his final pumps. When he reached the moment that made him fall apart, he shoved himself in hard and came, depositing his entire load deep inside me. "Fuck…" His ass tightened as he released, giving me all his seed. "Fuck, that's good." He stayed buried inside me as his cock twitched with its final squirts. It slowly started to soften until he was able to remove his cock easily, the come dripping between my legs right away. He rolled over and lay beside me, out of breath, tired, and also satisfied.

The area between my legs ached from the stretch, but I also felt a sense of peace wash over me, a calmness that could only be attributed to the intense pleasure I'd just received. His bed had never felt more comfortable, and I could easily drift off to sleep that very moment.

But we both had work in the morning, so I shouldn't stay. Last time, he let me stay over, but he quickly kicked me out the next day. That wasn't a fun memory.

Before I could get too tired, I sat up and felt his come slowly sink to my entrance. I still had my dress on, so I just had to hop out of the bed and grab my panties. I spotted them on the floor, so I stood up and felt his come shift inside me again, the heavy and warm substance that made me feel like a woman.

"What are you doing?" His deep voice filled the quiet and dark bedroom.

"Getting dressed."

"Why?" He sat up and looked at me, his disgruntled features visible in the lights of the city.

"Because if I don't put some panties on, I'm going to get your come everywhere. All over the elevator floor and the back seat of the car." I picked them up and pulled them on.

"If you keep talking like that, I'm going to fuck you again."

"It's just the truth."

He patted the bed beside him. "Get your ass back here."

"We have work in the morning."

"Then we'll go to work in the morning."

"I'll have to get up earlier so I can get back on time."

He patted the bed again, but this time harder. "Get your ass back over here now. Or I'll make you."

I stood with my hands on my hips. "Do you want me to stay?"

"Why else would I be acting barbaric right now?"

"Last time, you kicked me out pretty rudely."

"Well, it's not going to be like last time. So take off that dress and get into bed." He pulled the sheets back so we could both crawl inside. His dick had softened, but it was still impressive in size. It rested against his stomach, having the potential to balloon to twice its size in thirty seconds.

I pulled the dress over my head. "What am I going to wear?"

He nodded to his dresser. "There are t-shirts in there. Grab whatever one you want."

I helped myself to his clothes and pulled out a black t-shirt. The cotton surrounded me, smelling like laundry detergent. I moved back to bed and got under the covers beside him. "Your bed is comfy…"

"I'm comfier." He pulled me across the bed toward him so I was right against his chest. He hiked my leg over his waist so we could sleep close together, my tits against his hard chest. His hand slid under the cotton of my shirt so he could grip my waist as he closed his eyes.

I was tired a minute ago, but now I was wide awake. "Can I ask you something?"

"Yes." He rested his face close to mine, his brown eyes open.

"Am I the only woman you've slept with twice? Since Simone?"

He slightly cringed at the sound of her name. "Yes. In the last five years."

"So you've never wanted to sleep with your other lovers more than once?"

"I wouldn't call them lovers, just transactions. We weren't two people making love or fucking. It was just me taking their virginity as they lay there. They were compensated with cash, so lover isn't the right word."

"Fine. But I'm the only one?"

He nodded. "You're the only one."

"Why is that?" I'd run out on him twice, and instead of forgetting about me, he'd offered me more money. He negotiated with me when any other man would have forgotten me. "From the beginning, you've wanted me more than the others."

He considered my question for a long time before he verbalized a response. "I guess I respected you. You had nothing, but you continued to hold on to your virtue like it was worth more than all the money in the world. I was mean and aggressive with you, and you didn't want that to be your first time. So you turned me down…turned down all that cash. You have morals…and most people in this town don't. I guess I wanted to be what you wanted me to be. It made me patient and understanding. It made me gentle. It made me want you so bad that I was willing to do anything to have you."

I tamed this monster, made him feel gentle emotions for the first time in five years, maybe ever. I forced him to remember he had a soul, that women weren't just products on the shelf at a supermarket, but we had real feelings. The night he finally popped my cherry, he lit candles all over the room and sprinkled rose petals on the bed. The man I'd originally met never would have done those things. "You know what I think?"

"What?" His fingertips rubbed against the skin across my belly.

"I think you're finally moving on. I think you're finally letting the past go. I think you're finally starting to feel things again. It's been slow progress, but you've changed a lot since we met. That never would have happened if you weren't ready to move on."

He raised an eyebrow. "What does that mean?"

"You spent time with me for a month before we finally had sex. You've never done that before."

"So?"

"I think that means you're changing. You say you can't trust anyone again, but you obviously want to."

Instead of taking my words as a compliment like they were meant to be, they seemed to irritate him. "What did I tell you about analyzing me?"

"I'm not analyzing you—"

"That's exactly what you're doing. You're overthinking my behavior. The truth is, I don't know why I gave up a month of my life to take you to dinner and spend time with you. I wanted to sleep with you, and maybe having to work for it made it better. Now I paid for another three months of your time because I haven't stopped thinking about that cunt since the last time I had it. Maybe that means something…but maybe it doesn't. Maybe you're just the best sex I've ever had and that's the end of the story."

I didn't want to believe that. After the three months passed, we would have been seeing each other for nearly five months. That was a long time to be with the same person, especially for someone like him. He could pretend I meant nothing to him, but eventually, he would realize that wasn't the case. "I didn't mean to anger you."

"You didn't. I'm just frustrated. I hate it when people tell me how I feel."

"Sometimes it's hard to be objective when we're stuck in our own heads."

"And sometimes we see things that aren't really there." He gave me a look full of accusation.

It turned quiet, our romantic moment zapped away by the tensions between us. It wasn't my intention to stir up trouble. I just wanted Slate to realize he was letting go of his past, that he was moving forward with me without even noticing it.

Maybe he didn't want to realize it.

The tension only heightened until it became unbearable.

Perhaps I'd sabotaged our night. "I think I'm going to go…" I turned away to crawl out of bed.

He snatched me and pulled me back. "No."

"Really? I don't feel welcome here."

"Just because you piss me off doesn't mean I want you to leave." He hiked my leg back over his hip. "And when I piss you off, which I will, I hope you don't take off either."

"Depends on how pissed I am."

"Well, I'll try not to piss you off too much…even though I think you're cute when you're mad."

"Then you haven't seen me truly mad," I threatened.

He rubbed his nose against mine. "How about we stop talking about the future? How about we save this conversation for three months from now?"

It seemed like every time I brought it up, I made the problem worse. "Alright."

His fingers moved between my legs, and he rubbed my lips with his fingers. "Are you sore?"

"A bit."

"It'll get easier."

"Is it normal to be sore for a while?" I always thought it would hurt the first time, but then after that, it would feel normal. The second time hurt as much as the first.

"I think you're just really tight…and I'm larger than average."

"Sounds like we're a terrible match."

He continued to rub my entrance, soothing the pain with his touch. "No…I think we're perfect together."

23

Slate

My brother was getting married in two days.

In two days, he would throw his life away—and half of his portion of the company.

I knew she would divorce him quickly, take half of his income so she could have the glamorous life she wanted—without a husband. If she killed him, she could have half the company entirely.

I knew she was a bitch—but she wasn't that extreme.

The only reason I was going was because I had to. I wasn't in the wedding, thankfully. That would have been even more awkward. It was just my brother and Simone and two friends, along with my mom and Simone' parents. It would be on the beach in the Hamptons, a short drive away. Simone probably didn't want a big wedding because she wouldn't be married to him longer than a year, and that would just be bad publicity for her. Plus, it would be a waste of money. Maybe she would go big with her second marriage—with my brother's money.

I stared at the paperwork on my desk, stuff I was bringing to the meeting I had in fifteen minutes. Coen and Simone would be there, wrapping things up before they went on a short honeymoon in the Bahamas.

When they returned, it would be hell.

Jillian spoke into my intercom. "They're ready for you, sir."

"Thanks." I continued to sit there anyway, thinking about the woman who was occupying my bed. I never had women spend the night, but it seemed appropriate for her to stay there until morning. When she cuddled with me, she didn't make me hot. She didn't snore. And it was nice seeing her first thing in the morning.

With the exception of the way she analyzed me, she was wonderful company.

Now that she was back, I felt whole again.

Jillian spoke into my intercom again. "I apologize, sir. Miss Simone is getting—"

"I'll be right there, Jillian." I snatched the papers off my desk and left my office. Simone hadn't even married my brother yet, but she was trying to run the company like she was some kind of CEO.

Bitch.

I marched into the conference room and saw her sitting beside Coen, dressed in a black suit with large buttons in the front. She had short hair that was so short she couldn't pull it back, so she always left it down.

Once I stepped into the room, her smile disappeared, and she gave me an overtly disgruntled look. "Took you long enough."

I slammed the papers onto the desk before I took a seat. "I was working, not marching down the halls trying to *pretend* I was working." When I looked at my brother, I gave him an even angrier look, unable to believe this woman had turned him into the biggest pushover in the world. Men and women could be equals, but Coen let her run with the ball like some kind of idiot. She was the alpha—and he was the beta. It was fucking pathetic. "Running this company is about more than showing up to meetings with color-coded tabs in your folder. Never rush me again."

Simone twirled her pen in her fingertips, wearing a stoic expression but with a hint of rage in her eyes. "Coen, you're going to let him talk to me like that?"

"You bet your ass he is," I said before my brother could say anything. "Because he's the biggest pussy in the world—and we both know it. The man I used to know had a real sac and a tough spine. Now he's just a pathetic pushover."

Coen rose to that insult. "Shut the fuck up—"

"You shut the fuck up." I slammed my fist onto the table. "In two days, this cunt is going to have you by your balls—for good. I don't even want to help you anymore because you don't deserve it. When she rips out your heart and humiliates you in front of the whole world, I'll be laughing. I'll be laughing like everyone else."

Coen balled his hand into a fist as the cords in his neck thickened. He clearly wanted to strike me, but since I was much bigger, that would be a waste of time, not to mention, humiliating.

"Let's just do this shit." I opened my folder. "I've started negotiations near Jackson Hole. The property is ideal because it's within the national park at Yellowstone, and it also has stunning views. There's a lake nearby, so guests can look out their windows and see the buffalo with the naked eye. The property isn't nearly as expensive as some of our other resorts. If we start right away, we could have construction completed in eighteen months." I only looked at my brother because I refused to include her in the discussions.

"You think many people go to Jackson Hole?" Coen asked as he slowly started to calm down.

"There're limited resorts there, and every time I check availability, there's almost no vacancy—at any time of year. It'll be perfect for a cozy lodge, especially in the fall. In the summer, it'll do just as well because that's when it's the most popular."

Simone took notes as she listened.

I wanted to snatch the pen out of her hand and stab her in the neck with it.

Coen considered it for a long time. "It's not what we usually do, but it's not a bad idea."

"It's a great idea because it's guaranteed to do well. Acquiring land is difficult because it's a national park, but they've given us permission to build. We have to adhere to the environmental guidelines for clean energy and proper disposal, but that shouldn't be difficult. One of my architects found roof tiles that are solar panels. You can't even tell they're solar panels."

"But aren't they more expensive?"

I shrugged. "They require it."

Simone kept scribbling notes.

"I think it's a good idea," Coen said. "We should do it." He turned to Simone. "Babe, what do you think?"

I had to swallow the insult sitting on my tongue.

"Yes," Simone said. "I think it's a great investment and something we can promote to our existing clientele."

Our clientele? Fuck, I hated her. She took my virginity, my brother, and now she was trying to take my company. She did nothing to build it into the empire it was, but she got to call it hers, like she had ownership of it already. "Great. I just need a few signatures, and I'll get everything started." I pushed the pile of papers toward him, which were marked with tabs so he knew where to sign.

Like an idiot, he didn't read anything he was signing. He just added his signatures and the date.

Fucking stupid.

I pushed the paper to Simone. "Sign in the same places."

"Why?" Coen asked. "If we aren't married?"

"You'll be married in two days," I said. "We'll just have to go back and add her signatures later, and it'll be a pain. May as well just do it now."

Like she'd scored a victory, she smiled then added her signatures underneath Coen's.

She was also stupid.

The papers were returned to me.

I quickly placed them in the folder. "I guess I'll see you on Saturday."

"Bringing that brunette?" Simone asked as she watched me rise from the chair.

"Why?" I asked. "Jealous?"

"I think you're the one who's jealous." She moved her hand across the table and rested it on Coen's.

He squeezed her hand in return.

Why was my family so fucked up? "Yes, I'm bringing her."

WHEN I LEFT THE OFFICE, I went straight to Monroe's apartment.

She opened the door after I knocked, wearing a pink dress with a white cardigan. Summer was officially over, but she dressed like she wasn't ready to say goodbye. "What a nice surprise."

I stepped over the threshold and kissed her on the mouth, greeting her the way a man greeted his woman. I sucked her bottom lip then gave her some of my tongue, wanting to blow off steam after the shitty day I'd had.

Her hands immediately unbuttoned the front of my shirt and got my belt undone. "You're frisky today."

Just pissed off. "My brother is getting married on Saturday. Would you like to come with me?" I hadn't intended to bring her because the thought hadn't crossed my mind. Mother would ask a million questions and pry into my personal life. But I didn't want to give

Simone the impression I was alone and lonely. I had a woman a million times better than she ever was. Not only was Monroe beautiful, she had a heart that dwarfed everyone else's.

"Really?" she asked, clearly surprised by the request. "Yeah, sure. I just hope I have something to wear."

"It's on the beach, so anything will be fine."

"But you guys are like billionaires…"

"Trust me, anything is fine." My hands peeled her cardigan off her body then I moved to the slender straps over her shoulders. I pushed them down so the thin material would slide off her body, revealing her boobs with taped-down nipples.

I eyed them and tried not to smile.

She quickly covered them and pulled the tape loose. "You didn't catch me at my finest hour."

"I'm not judging you." My hands palmed her free tits, and I swiped my thumb over her nipples, feeling them pebble at my touch. "So, you'll come with me?"

"Of course. Isn't your mom gonna be there?"

I nodded. "Yes. And she'll be obsessed with you. She already asked me a million questions about you."

"How does she know about me in the first place?"

"She knows I took you to that charity event." I backed her up toward the bedroom in the corner, where her small queen bed had rumpled sheets because she hadn't bothered making the bed that morning. When we reached the foot of the bed, I pulled her thong down. After dealing with bullshit all afternoon, I just wanted to fuck pussy.

Her fingers finished my buttons before she removed

my tie. She looked me in the eye with a slight smile on her lips, her fingers working my clothing until most of it was on the ground. She popped the button of my slacks and undid the zipper so they would fall to the floor. "You seem stressed."

"I am."

Her hands moved up my bare chest as she rose on tiptoes to give me a kiss. It was soft and sweet, full of her vanilla innocence. Her lips moved quicker, and then she gave me her small tongue, keeping the pace slow even though the passion had increased.

Then she abruptly pulled away…and lowered herself to her knees.

I stopped breathing once I saw her face right in front of my dick

"Maybe I can help you relax…" She gripped my thighs and then pressed her lips against my sac. She dropped her kisses everywhere, sliding her tongue across the textured skin as she felt my balls intimately. She kissed and sucked, giving them the same attention my cock always received. Then she grabbed my shaft and pointed the crown right at her mouth. She stuck out her tongue, flattened it, and then started to move in.

Jesus Christ.

Her throat slowly covered my length, her tongue acting as a buffer to keep me slick and protected. She moved as far as she could go without coughing and then slowly pulled me out again. Like she wasn't in a hurry to speed this up, she kept moving at that pace, letting her throat get used to having a huge dick inside it.

"Look at me." My hand moved into her hair as I slowly thrust into her mouth.

Her eyes flicked to mine.

I wanted to deep-throat her good and hard, but this woman was too inexperienced for that. She liked things slow and gentle—for now. And I wanted her to keep breathing, so I let her do most of the leading. But when I saw those eyes look into mine, I wanted to come on the spot. "Yes…just like that."

COEN AND SIMONE were getting married at sunset, so I didn't need to leave my penthouse until Saturday morning. Since it was a beach wedding, I intended to wear slacks and a collared shirt with sandals. They couldn't expect me to wear a suit and tie under such conditions.

I picked up Monroe next.

She wore a beautiful purple dress with her hair in big curls. One side was pinned back, so most of her curls were situated on one side of her head. It was a hairstyle I hadn't seen her wear before, but I liked it. She wore a gold necklace around her throat and flats that would be appropriate for the sand.

"You look beautiful." I kissed her before I opened the back door for her, taking her bag from her.

"Thank you. You do too."

"I look beautiful?" I said with a chuckle.

"Yes," she said with a straight face. "You're a very beautiful man." She got into the car.

Once I was in the back seat beside her, we left Manhattan and began the drive toward the tip of Long Island. After we were out of the city, the traffic cleared up, and we started to cruise.

She looked at the ocean, her eyes lit up with joy. "At least it'll be a beautiful wedding. It's perfect weather."

"Yeah." I didn't give a damn about the weather. It could rain for all I cared.

"So…what do I tell your mother?"

"About what?" I asked.

"Us. What if she asks?"

"She's not gonna ask that. I mean, she'll ask me that but not you."

"You said your mother is nosy…"

"Then if she does ask, just say we're seeing each other casually."

"Alright." She crossed her legs and looked out the window again, looking stunning as the sunlight hit her just right.

It was unlike me to bring a woman to a family event since I'd never done it before, but having Monroe there would make this trip less of a nightmare. I would watch karma punish my brother for what he did to me—even though it seemed like too harsh of a punishment. We would have dinner, and I would be on my best behavior because I was obligated to keep my mouth shut for twelve hours. Having Monroe there would help with that. When I was the most irritated, she could soothe my rage. And that night, my cock would be balls deep in her pussy, so I had something to look forward to.

"Are you doing okay?" she asked.

"Yes. I'm fine."

"When your jaw gets tight like that, it either means you're turned on or angry."

"Well, you're in the car, so I would say I'm turned on."

She glanced at my lap. "If you were, your hard-on would be unmistakable. So you're just pissed."

"I'm not looking forward to this. I'll leave it at that."

"Because of her? Or because of him?"

Because of everything. I hated my brother for what he did to me, but I didn't think he deserved this betrayal. Simone was evil, and it shocked me that she'd made it this far in her life. She managed to keep tricking and manipulating people. When would her lies catch up to her? "Both."

WE ARRIVED AT THE BEACH, and I introduced Monroe to my mother. "Monroe, this is Elizabeth Remington."

"Such a pleasure to meet you." Monroe beamed as she shook my mother's hand. "Slate always speaks highly of you."

Mother laughed. "Except when he doesn't. But I'm grateful he has anything nice to say at all." She smiled at Monroe then kissed me on the cheek. "You look very handsome, honey. But I think you look more handsome because you finally have a beautiful woman on your arm." She turned back to Monroe. "And you're definitely beautiful, dear." She grabbed her arm and gave it an affectionate squeeze.

"Thank you," Monroe said, visibly touched by the compliment.

"So, how's Coen?" I asked, feeling obligated to voice the question.

"He's fine. Perfectly calm."

"That's too bad." He really had no idea what was about to hit him.

Mother patted me on the shoulder. "Being a mother taught me that you can't control your kids. You guide them as much as you can, but in the end, they make their own decisions—even when they are young. They're going to make terrible mistakes that will break your heart, but you have to let them make them—and let them learn."

Couldn't he make a better mistake? Like buying a sports car when he needed an SUV?

"Let it be." She guided us to the row of chairs in the front. "Let's take a seat."

I sat beside Monroe and placed my hand on her thigh.

She circled her arm through mine and held on to it like a pillow.

The ceremony started minutes later, and Simone's father walked her down the aisle. I noticed her parents didn't say anything to me even though I had dated their daughter. I also noticed the genuine love on my brother's face as he watched Simone come toward him in her wedding dress.

Poor bastard.

Cherry Popper

Simone kissed her father before she joined hands with my brother, looking like a woman genuinely in love.

All bullshit.

Then the pastor began the ceremony—and my brother signed over his soul to the devil.

WE HAD a private dinner together at the hotel, sitting on the balcony overlooking the water. Coen and Simone sat in the center of the long table, while everyone else was gathered around the sides. There were a few friends and other family members.

I didn't bother mingling. I preferred the company of Monroe and my mother.

"Her gown is beautiful," Mother said. "Truly."

"It is," Monroe said in agreement, complimenting the woman I despised.

My mother turned back to Monroe. "How did you two meet?"

Monroe didn't know what to say, so she opened her mouth while she tried to find an answer.

"In a bar," I lied. "She was sitting alone. I took one look at her and went for it."

"The rest is history," Monroe added, going along with the lie.

"You're very cute together," Mother said. "I saw pictures of you two online. You seem very happy." She turned her head to look at me, giving me a focused expression.

"It's pretty casual," Monroe said. "But Slate is a

great guy, and I've enjoyed spending time with him. He can be a little grizzled at times, but once you peel away that hard exterior, he's a good guy underneath."

"I couldn't agree more," Mother said. She looked directly into my eyes. "If you find someone who likes you for you, then consider yourself lucky. And it seems like this young lady accepts you for who you are."

More than she could ever understand. "Yes, Monroe is lovely." My arm rested over the back of her chair. "Smart. Funny. Lovely. And she doesn't put up with my shit…even though I wish she would sometimes."

"Never." Monroe smiled before she took a drink.

Mother watched us together, her eyes shrewd and observant. She said nothing more about our relationship but continued to sit there quietly, like she was thinking a million things at once.

THE EVENING FINALLY ENDED, and Coen and Simone left in a limo for the airport. The other guests said goodnight and headed to their hotel rooms.

Our room was right in front of the elevator, so I told Monroe to meet me at the room while I walked my mother to her room on the opposite side of the resort. It was almost two in the morning, and I didn't want my mother walking outside the building alone.

I escorted her through the gardens toward the second building.

"I like her a lot, Slate."

I kept my hands in my pockets as I walked. "I figured you would."

"She's perfect."

"I think so too, but you hardly know her."

"She's easy to read—and she cares about you a lot."

I already knew that. She wouldn't put up with my bullshit otherwise. "Don't get too attached."

"You'd better get more attached," she snapped. "That woman is nothing like Simone. She's warm, friendly, and genuinely kind. You shouldn't let the past affect your future so much, not when you have a good woman right in front of you."

I decided to change the subject. "Where are Simone and Coen going on their honeymoon again?"

My mother didn't fall for it. "You'd better give this woman a chance. Life is short, and you don't want to waste time being lonely and depressed when there's a good woman out there. You wouldn't have brought her here in the first place if you didn't adore her."

"I never said I didn't."

"Well, you fight for her." Mother stopped when she reached her doorstep. "Don't do something stupid like push her away. I know you, Slate. You've been wasting your time with women who don't matter. You finally find someone you actually like, so you should be everything she deserves. Otherwise…" She snapped her fingers. "She'll replace you like that."

I sighed but kept my annoyance in check. "I'll consider what you said."

"Good." She kissed me on the cheek. "Thank you

for walking me to my room. You're always a gentleman."

"Because you're always a lady."

"Monroe is a lady too. So you should be nothing but a gentleman to her."

I WALKED into the room and found her already in her thong. She'd shed her dress and hung it up in the closet in the living room. She had the sexiest curves and the softest skin. She didn't even understand just how beautiful she truly was.

"Your mom is wonderful."

"You're just saying that because she liked you." I unbuttoned my shirt and stripped it off my body.

She shrugged. "I'm sure that has a lot to do with it."

I undid my belt as I walked to her, seeing her in nothing but panties. "You know what we talked about during that entire walk?"

"Me, I'm guessing?"

I undid my slacks and let them fall to the ground. "Yes."

"And…?"

"She likes you—a bit too much."

"Wow, it's the first time I've met a man's mother, and I rocked it." She chuckled then tucked her hair behind her ear.

"Yes, you did." My hands moved to her hips so my fingers could feel the lacy fabric. "Thanks for coming with me to this. You could have done something better than witness my family drama."

"What are friends for?" She rubbed her hands up my chest. "I figured I would get a night of good sex out of it."

"You definitely will."

"Then maybe I did this for my own selfish reasons." She moved in and kissed me on the chest, her plump lips sticking to my skin slightly as she pulled away. "By the way, you did well today. I know this couldn't have been easy for you…watching your brother fall for her schemes."

It wasn't easy at all. It was my job to protect him, but I couldn't. Now I had to watch him make an idiot out of himself for the world to see. Simone would have humiliated both of the Remington brothers once she was finished with us. "No, it wasn't. But it was a lot easier with you here." My hands snaked up her ribs, and I rested my forehead against hers, feeling the chemistry between our bodies without actually igniting the fire.

Maybe in three months this would burn out. Or maybe in three months I wouldn't be able to let her go. I had no idea what I was doing, but I was still going to do it. Because letting her go just wasn't an option for me.

I didn't want anyone else to have her.

To have my woman.

Also by Victoria Quinn

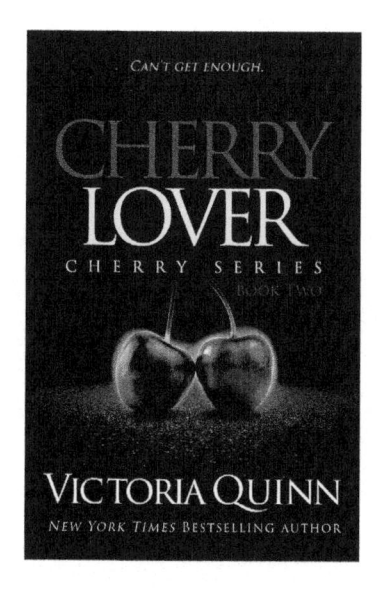

Order Now

Printed in Great Britain
by Amazon